P9-CLD-543

MIND OVER MURDER

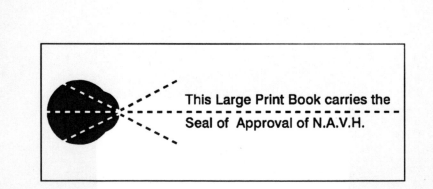

MIND OVER MURDER

ALLISON KINGSLEY

WHEELER PUBLISHING
A part of Gale, Cengage Learning

GALE
CENGAGE Learning·

Detroit • New York • San Francisco • New Haven, Conn • Waterville, Maine • London

GALE
CENGAGE Learning·

LIBRARY OF CONGRESS CATALOGING-IN-PUBLICATION DATA

Kingsley, Allison.
    Mind over murder / by Allison Kingsley. — Large print ed.
      p. cm. — (Wheeler Publishing large print cozy mystery)
    "A Raven's Nest bookstore mystery."
    ISBN-13: 978-1-4104-4536-0 (pbk.)
    ISBN-10: 1-4104-4536-4 (pbk.)
    1. Bookstores—Fiction. 2. Precognition—Fiction. 3. Large type books.
  I. Title.
PR9199.3.K44228M56 2012
813'.54—dc23   2011049661

Published in 2012 by arrangement with The Berkley Publishing Group, a member of Penguin Group (USA) Inc.

Printed in the United States of America
1 2 3 4 5   16 15 14 13 12
FD069

To my husband, Bill,
whose patience and understanding
under the circumstances have been
incredible. You are a joy and a blessing.

ACKNOWLEDGMENTS

Many thanks to my editor, Michelle Vega, for all your hard work, great ideas and infinite patience. Your efforts are truly appreciated.

Grateful thanks to my agent, Paige Wheeler, for steering me in the right direction and for being there for me when I need you. You know what that means to me.

To my good friends Sam Willey and Mr. Bill, for assisting me with my research and for all the wonderful pics of the Maine coast. They are invaluable.

1

"Stephanie Quinn Dowd, you've got to be kidding!" Clara Quinn stared at her cousin's serious face and suppressed an urge to laugh. "I've never worked in a bookstore. Or any store for that matter. Why in the world would you want me to manage yours?"

The other woman puffed a strand of fair hair out of her eyes and dumped a pile of books onto the counter in front of her.

"Because you're smart, you're personable and you have a degree in literature. I need someone for the afternoon shift. Twelve till eight. I'll be here most of the day. Besides, you need a job, and I desperately need help. Look at this!" She swept a hand around her in a wide arc.

Clara gazed around at the rows of shelves loaded with books, the tables displaying classic titles, the posters on the walls and the cozy corner with its deep armchairs and large coffee urn.

It didn't look much different from the last time she'd seen it, shortly after Stephanie had opened the store three months ago. Except for the sinister-looking stuffed raven perched on a light fixture and the sparkling colored crystals slowly spinning from the ceiling on golden cords. Oh, and maybe the life-size figure of a fortune-teller hovering over a crystal ball. Clara grinned. "I didn't know you still had Madam Sophia."

Stephanie's laugh seemed to echo along the shelves. "Do you remember when we rescued her from that awful carnival?"

"How could I forget? I was the one who climbed up that huge pile of trash to get to her."

"We were so excited. Then my mom saw us carrying it upstairs to my room and just about went berserk."

Clara shook her head. "Poor Madam Sophia. Relegated to a cold, drafty garage."

"We didn't sleep all night worrying about her."

Clara joined in her cousin's laughter. "Well, she looks healthy enough now."

Stephanie's grin vanished as the sound of angry voices erupted on the street outside. "What's going on out there?"

"Sounds like someone's upset about

something." Clara glanced at the old-fashioned grandfather clock by the door. "I'd better get going. I'm supposed to be looking for an apartment."

"Wait! Are you going to help me out or not?"

Clara paused, reluctant to give an answer. It was true she needed a job. She just wasn't sure this one would be a good idea. For a lot of reasons.

"Please?" Stephanie looked worried. "Ever since I started serving coffee and snacks in the Reading Nook, we've been swamped with customers. Molly's been doing the afternoon shift now that Jonathon has gone back to college, but I really need her here in the mornings, and I must have someone reliable to take over for her in the afternoons."

"Have you tried advertising the position?"

"Of course, but this is a small town, and it's hard finding someone suitable for the job. My mom's been taking care of the kids while I'm here, but once school starts next week she'll be back at work, and I can't rely on George; he has his own job to worry about. I'm pretty desperate, Clara."

Again Clara struggled with her conscience. "I'd like to, Stephanie, but I don't really have the time." Seeing her cousin's face freeze, she hurried on. "I'm still getting settled in, I'm looking for an apartment and I have to find a teaching position —"

Again the raised voices interrupted her. Glancing at the window, she puffed out her breath. From the day they were born, just two months apart, she and Stephanie had shared everything from baby formulas and childhood nightmares to adolescent dreams. Since neither of them had siblings, they'd turned to each other, forming a sisterhood that had lasted thirty years and would continue, Clara hoped, for as long as they lived. They trusted and relied on each other as only close family can.

She would do almost anything for Stephanie, and now her cousin needed her. She just couldn't see any way she could refuse without seeming selfish and heartless.

Swallowing her reservations, she held up her hands. "All right. I'll do it. On the condition that it's only until you find someone permanent."

"Great!" Stephanie's face glowed with excitement. "Can you start tomorrow? Perhaps come in a little early? I could use the extra help for the sale."

Clara gave her a reluctant nod. "Okay."

"Thanks. It'll be fun; you'll see."

"I'm not so sure." Clara waved a hand at

the shelves. "You know how I feel about all this magic and spiritual stuff."

"I know you used to love it as much as I do. Until you found out you have the Quinn Sense."

And there it was. Clara waited a full five seconds before answering. "We've talked about this before. That's why I left Finn's Harbor in the first place. To get away from all that."

"And now you're back." Stephanie came out from behind the counter and laid a hand on her cousin's arm. "I don't know why you're so determined to ignore the fact that you have the gift. It's a family heritage, and I'd give anything to have it."

"I'd give anything if you had it instead of me."

"I know. That's what makes it so frustrating." Stephanie dropped her hand and frowned at the window as the sound of angry voices outside intensified. "I'd better go and see what all that is about."

Heading for the door, she threw words over her shoulder. "Be a dear before you leave and go to the stockroom for me? I need the box marked "High School." The books are required reading for the students, and I need to get the rest of these tables set up if we're going to start our back-to-school

13

event today." She disappeared, leaving her cousin no chance to answer.

Shaking her head, Clara set off down one of the aisles to the back of the store. Talk of the gift had unsettled her, as it always did. Most members of the Quinn family had some psychic ability, and she wasn't happy about being included in that favored circle. In fact, it had become such a burden that she'd left Maine in the hopes that she could forget all about the family curse, as she called it, and feel less of a freak.

At first, in the excitement of attending college in New York, she'd managed to ignore the odd moments when she could read people's hidden thoughts or have a momentary glimpse into the future. For a while she'd almost felt normal.

But life in New York was so different from the life she'd left behind in Finn's Harbor. She missed her family and friends, and Stephanie most of all. Each time she'd visited, it had gotten harder to leave.

There was a time when she'd resented the small-town community, where it seemed that everyone knew everybody's business. She'd found out, however, that a big city could be incredibly lonely, and true friends were hard to make. In her need for companionship, she'd sometimes been too quick to trust, and it had backfired on her. Big time.

Coming back to Finn's Harbor, however, meant facing the same demons that had sent her away in the first place. Pushing open the stockroom door, Clara sighed. All she could hope was that she'd made the right decision to come back to her hometown. Only time would tell.

Inside the crowded room, she gazed in awe at the piles of boxes stacked against the walls. It looked like she'd arrived in the nick of time. Stephanie sure had her hands full, now that the Raven's Nest bookstore had become one of the most popular social centers in town.

Catching sight of the bust of a man, she moved over to the table to inspect it more closely. The face looked vaguely familiar, and she studied it for a moment before bending closer to read the inscription. Of course. Edgar Allan Poe. She should have guessed. Stephanie crammed her shelves with anything remotely connected to the author.

Gently, she laid a hand on the smooth surface of the head. So many nights when she and her cousin were kids, they'd spent sleepovers watching horror movies and pretending to be psychics.

They'd filled hours reading each other's

palms and predicting wild, adventurous futures for themselves. They'd eagerly discussed how they would use the Quinn Sense once they developed it.

Even then she'd felt uneasy about it, though she'd never admitted as much to Stephanie. Her cousin had loved every creepy moment, while Clara had been scared they would conjure up some terrible evil spirit who would steal their souls.

At first, when she'd realized she had inherited the family's psychic powers, it had seemed thrilling and even empowering, but as time went by, the voices she heard became an intrusion. It hadn't helped matters to learn that somehow the gift had bypassed Stephanie.

Clara sighed and patted the bust. How ironic that she should be the one to inherit the Quinn Sense, as everyone called it, instead of her spook-happy cousin.

The sudden tingling in her hand took her by surprise. She snatched it back as a wave of darkness seemed to cloud her mind. Evil. She could sense it in the room, cold and menacing.

For a moment she felt rooted to the spot, unable to move a muscle. Then she forced her mind to clear, and everything settled back into place.

Heart still pounding, she quickly scanned the boxes until she found the one marked "High School" in uneven black letters. She grabbed it up and charged out the door, not even bothering to close it behind her.

She reached the counter just as Stephanie walked in through the front door, followed closely by a young woman with tangled red hair and flushed cheeks. Both of them stared as Clara came to a halt, breathless and shaking.

Her cousin was the first to speak. "Are you okay? You're looking a bit weird."

Clara gulped in air. Glancing out the window, she could see Ana Jordan, the owner of the stationer's next door, glaring at the bookstore, her short, chubby body still in fighting mode with feet planted apart and hands on her hips. The furious woman threw her hands in the air, then ran them through her cropped bleached hair before turning and stomping back to her store.

"I'm fine." Clara gestured at the window. I thought I heard someone yelling."

"You did." The redhead held out her hand. "I'm Molly Owens, Steph's assistant. I've heard a lot about you."

"All of it disgusting, I suppose." Clara shook the firm fingers.

Molly grinned. "Let's just say you two

must have had a dynamite childhood."

Clara gave her cousin a sharp glance. Stephanie had promised long ago not to tell anyone, including their own family, that her cousin had the gift. She was reassured by Stephanie's firm shake of her head and answered Molly with a smile. "You've got that right."

"Well, Steph told me you'll be working here." Molly tilted her head to one side, her green eyes sparkling with mischief. "I have to say, it'll be fab to have someone here tall enough to reach the top shelves."

Stephanie laughed and walked over to the counter. "Just don't ask her how tall she is. The kids in high school drove her nuts with that question."

"Oh, bummer." Molly paused. "So, how tall are you, then?"

"Tall enough to thump you on the head if you ask that question again." Clara glanced at the window again. "So what was all the shouting about out there?"

"Oh, that was me." Molly sighed. "I was screaming at that old bat next door. I tell you, that woman is nuts. You know her, don't you?"

"Of course I know her." Clara rolled her eyes at Stephanie. "Most of these shops have changed hands so often I don't know anyone anymore, but Jordan's has been here since we were kids. Is Ana still causing trouble for everyone?"

Stephanie shrugged. "Nothing we can't handle."

Molly made a guttural sound of disgust. "That woman should be run out of town. She hates Steph, she hates the bookstore, she hates the fact that we're successful and she'd do anything to shut us down."

Clara stared at her cousin. "Really? What's her problem?"

"She says I'm poisoning young minds with my occult books and turning our children into demons."

"Whoa, heavy stuff." Clara nodded at the nearest table. "Those don't look like occult books."

"They're not!" Molly's cheeks turned red again as she gestured at the tables. "Look at the titles. They're books the high school asked us to carry, and what about those?" She pointed to several rows of colorful hardbacks. "Craft books and cookbooks. There's lots of choices, and it's not like we're forcing people to buy the occult stuff."

"There's a lot of interest in it right now, though," Stephanie put in. "I'm not endangering anyone — I'm just supplying what the public wants."

"Yeah, well, Ana doesn't think you have any right to do that." Molly jerked her hand at the window again. "She keeps putting up signs advertising Big Books, that new chain bookstore that opened up last year. She's doing her best to put us out of business. I saw the poster and tore it down, and of course, she saw me do it. She came screaming out of the store, and she's like, 'I'll have you arrested!' and I'm like, 'Just try it, you old witch, and I'll burn your broomstick and you along with it.' "

"I told you just to ignore her." Stephanie picked up a pile of books and hurried over to one of the tables.

"If you ignore her, she'll get what she wants and shut you down. You have to *do* something about that woman." Molly turned to Clara, green eyes pleading. "You tell her."

"She has a point," Clara said mildly.

"I know what I'd like to do," Stephanie muttered, "but I can't afford any trouble. Not today." She carefully stood an opened book on top of the pile. "We have teenagers coming into this store today for our back-to-school sale. The last thing I need is a screaming match with Ana Jordan."

Molly muttered something under her breath. "If you won't do anything, then I will. I love this job, and I'm not going to let a miserable old hag take it away from me."

"Well, I appreciate you coming in early to help." Stephanie hurried back to the counter for more books. "I'm going to need more boxes from the stockroom. I'm counting on this sale to buy school clothes for my children."

Molly sighed. "I'm going. But don't think I'm going to forget about it. Ana Jordan has a nasty shock coming her way, sooner or later."

She rushed off toward the back of the store, leaving Stephanie to stare after her with a worried frown. "That girl is a good worker, but she's got a temper that would curl the devil's toes."

Clara laughed. "I seem to have heard that somewhere before."

"You know as well as I do that I've gotten a lot better at controlling my temper." Stephanie carried more books over to the table. "Though my kids do know not to push me too far."

"I bet they do. Well, I'd better get over to the rental agency." Clara headed for the door. "They've probably rented that apartment by now."

"You don't like living with Aunt Jessie?"

Clara hesitated. "It's okay, I guess. It's

just that I'm used to living on my own. So is my mother. She's gotten a lot more independent since Dad died."

"I know. It's sad. They were so happy together. I miss Uncle David and his silly jokes."

"We all miss him." Clara pulled the door open, jingling the bell and letting in the warm sunshine.

"Clara? Did anything . . . weird happen in the stockroom?"

Clara paused, one hand on the door handle. "Weird?"

"You know. *Weird.*" Stephanie looked uncomfortable. "You had that odd look on your face you always used to get when —"

"Nothing happened." Clara made an effort to soften her tone. "Good luck with the sale. I'll see you in the morning." She didn't wait for an answer.

Once outside, she pulled in a deep breath of the fresh, salty air. Main Street stretched ahead of her for several blocks, sloping down toward the harbor.

In summertime, the town was always crowded with tourists, and today was no exception. On either side, people strolled along in front of the quaint shop windows, peering under the colorful striped awnings at souvenirs, antiques, artwork and beach supplies.

At the bottom of the hill, boats bobbed around in the bay, their white sails gleaming in the sun, while behind them a thin line of fluffy white clouds separated the pale blue sky from the deeper blue of the ocean.

Clara's heart warmed at the sight. This was what she'd missed so much — this little town with its friendly people; its unique little shops and charming, narrow streets; the bustling activity of the picturesque bay. Here she could find peace and put all the problems of New York behind her. This was Finn's Harbor, Maine, and this was where she belonged.

Glancing across the street, she saw a man standing in front of the hardware store, one hand shading his face as he gazed at something farther down the street.

He didn't seem to be a tourist, and Clara stared hard for a long moment, trying to recognize the rugged features that were half hidden behind his hand.

Deciding that she didn't know him, she was about to turn away when he twisted his head in her direction. He apparently realized she'd been staring at him, as he touched his fingers to his forehead in a mock salute.

Embarrassed, she ducked her head and

took off down the hill. Things had changed a lot since she'd left, twelve years ago. People had gone, and others moved in, and although she'd come back to visit several times every year, it wasn't the same as living there. She felt like a stranger now in her own hometown.

She wondered if the man across the street was a stranger or if he had lived there long enough to become a familiar member of the community. Then, wondering why on earth she was still thinking about him, she headed for the rental agency.

The following morning, Clara arrived on the doorstep of the Raven's Nest just as Stephanie was opening up the store. "I couldn't sleep," she explained, in answer to her cousin's raised eyebrows. "I thought I might as well come down early and give you a hand."

"Well, good. That will give me time to show you the ropes." Stephanie walked in ahead of her. "It will be a long day, though, and you'll probably regret coming in early by the time it's over. Molly won't be here for another hour. She stayed late last night to clean up, and I told her to sleep in. As you can see," she said and flapped her hand at the neat tables, "she did a great job."

"She sure did." Clara studied the stack of books on the table closest to her. "You should have called me. I could have helped. I wasn't doing anything."

"Did you find an apartment?"

"Nope. The one I saw was too small and didn't have a dishwasher. I've got to have some place to hide my dirty dishes."

"You only saw one apartment?"

Clara made a face. "This is Finn's Harbor. There's not a lot of rentals to choose from."

"Well, it's not New York, I give you that." Stephanie took a bunch of keys out of her purse and unlocked the cash register. "You'll just have to be less fussy about where you live."

"After looking at what's available out there, my mother's house is beginning to look a lot more comfortable. Even with her in it."

Stephanie laughed. "You'll be good for each other. Now come over here, and I'll show you how to ring up purchases."

Clara did her best to remember everything, jotting down notes as Stephanie explained her duties. The next half hour passed quickly, and by the time they were done, Clara felt reasonably confident she could handle anything, barring an unforeseen emergency.

"You can always call me if you're in doubt," Stephanie told her as she closed the file that held customers' new-book reservations. "I can be down here in a few minutes if you need me."

"I'll be fine," Clara assured her. She looked around, smiling as her glance fell on Madame Sophia. "I think this will be fun."

"I hope so. I want you to enjoy working here; then, maybe you'll stay." Stephanie grinned. "Now, I need you to go to the stockroom. The copies of Wayne Lester's new astrology book came in yesterday, and we need to get them out on the shelves. A lot of customers are waiting for that book."

At the mention of the stockroom, Clara felt a stab of uneasiness. She nodded, carefully keeping her expression blank.

Her cousin, however, knew her too well. "What's the matter?" Stephanie frowned. "Am I being too bossy?"

That made Clara smile. "You've always been bossy, but it's okay. You're the boss. You're entitled." Before Stephanie could probe anymore, she took off down the aisle and headed for the stockroom.

The disturbing sensation she'd felt the day before came back to haunt her as she opened the door. It didn't mean anything, she assured herself. She had moments like that all the time. Most of the time they went away without her ever knowing what was behind them. This was just one of those times. Even so, she braced herself as she pushed open the door and flipped on the light.

She had taken only two steps into the room when she saw the huddled figure on the floor. Shock slammed into her chest, making it hard to breathe. She tried to shout for Stephanie, but no sound would come out of her mouth.

She took a wobbly step or two forward and uttered a whimper of horror. The shattered pieces of Edgar Allan Poe's bust were scattered on the floor. In the center of them, Ana Jordan lay face-up, a puddle of dark blood spreading out from under her head.

2

Less than ten minutes later, Finn's Harbor's police chief climbed out of his car in front of the Raven's Nest. Clara recognized the stocky figure the moment she spotted him through the window.

Standing next to her behind the counter, Stephanie uttered a faint moan. "What are we going to do? We're supposed to open in half an hour."

"The customers will just have to wait until all this is over, that's all." Clara squeezed her cousin's hand. It felt cold, and Stephanie's face was drawn with shock.

Clara wasn't feeling so hot herself. Her stomach felt so messed up she was sure she'd never be able to eat with enjoyment again. The doorbell jangled, frying her already shattered nerves as the big man in uniform walked in.

Chief Dan Petersen had the kind of round face that always seemed to be smiling, though his blue eyes were shrewd and piercing, and missed very little. He was a jovial man, but he kept a firm hand over the officers who worked under him, and Clara had always admired that.

She didn't know the young officer who followed the chief, but Stephanie murmured a greeting to him as they paused in front of the counter. "Hi, Dan; hello, Tim. This is so horrible. I can't believe it."

Dan flicked a glance at Clara. "Guess you found the body, right?"

Clara swallowed, shut the memory out of her mind and nodded.

"Touch anything?"

"No, sir. I took one look and got out of there."

Dan nudged the young man standing next to him. "Let's take a look."

Clara watched them disappear down the aisle, shuddering as she envisioned the scene that awaited them. "Who do you think could have done such a thing?"

Stephanie rubbed her shoulders as if she were cold. "I don't know. Ana wasn't well liked, and she was always causing trouble, but I don't know anyone who would have wanted her dead."

"Well, apparently someone did. That bust didn't just fall on her head. What was she doing in your stockroom, anyway?"

"I don't know. Molly made that bust. She'd left it in the stockroom to dry. We were going to put it in the window. She'll be real upset that it's broken."

"Not to mention that it killed your neighbor," Clara said dryly.

"Well, of course." Stephanie opened the drawer beneath the counter and shut it again. "I didn't mean . . ."

"You didn't mean what?"

The gruff voice made them both jump. Clara gave the police chief a weak smile. He walked quietly for a big man. "She meant that Molly will be real upset about Ana."

The chief gave her a long look. "Where is Molly?"

Stephanie glanced at the tall clock. "She should be here soon."

The screeching of tires outside made them all turn to the window. An ambulance had pulled up, and two men in white coats jumped out and opened the back doors. They pulled out a gurney and wheeled it across the sidewalk as Dan strode to the door and opened it.

"Back room," he said briefly, before they could speak. "Don't touch anything until the doc gets here."

The two men nodded and wheeled the

squeaky stretcher down the aisle to the stockroom.

The door opened once more, and a breathless voice asked, "Who's sick?" Molly bounded into the shop, purse slung over her shoulder, eyes wide and hair flying.

Stephanie hurried out from behind the counter and took hold of Molly's hand. "There's been an accident," she said quietly. "It's Ana Jordan. Molly, I'm afraid she's dead."

Molly's eyebrows leapt up and down. "Dead?"

"Dead," echoed Dan, walking forward. "And it was no accident."

Molly stared at him. "What do you mean?"

"She's in the stockroom. Someone bashed her head in with a statue," Dan said bluntly.

Molly seemed unable to speak for a moment, her mouth opening and shutting as if gasping for air. Then she turned to Stephanie, her eyes wide and pleading. "Is it true? This isn't a joke?"

Stephanie sounded tearful when she answered. "It was your bust of Edgar, Molly. Someone used it to . . ." she choked, and put a hand over her mouth.

Clara rushed over to her. "We're all upset

right now. Come and sit down until you feel better."

"I can't sit down," Stephanie wailed. "It's Saturday. Everyone comes early on a Saturday. I have to open the store in fifteen minutes."

"Nobody's coming in here until we've finished the investigation." Dan walked over to the door and twisted the lock. "Now, everybody calm down. I need to ask you all some questions." He turned to Clara. "You first. Tell me exactly what you saw when you went into the stockroom this morning."

Clara shakily described the scene as best she could, while behind her, Molly whispered something to Stephanie.

The chief listened gravely; then, when she was done, he looked at her cousin. "Any idea why Ana was in your stockroom last night?"

Stephanie shook her head. "I have absolutely no idea." She turned to Molly. "Did you let Ana into the stockroom?"

Molly's eyes widened. "Of course not! I don't know how she got in there."

Dan grunted something under his breath. "Well, there's no sign of a break-in. The door was securely locked when you got here this morning?"

Stephanie sounded hoarse when she answered. "Yes, I unlocked it myself."

"You locked up last night before you left?"

"Molly did. I left around three yesterday afternoon."

The chief turned to Molly, who seemed to be having trouble looking him in the eye. "What about you? What time did *you* leave?"

Molly started to speak, paused some more, then blurted out, "About eight-thirty or so. I wanted to leave the place tidy for when Steph came in this morning. So I cleaned up before I left."

"You locked both doors before you left?"

"The back door is always kept locked unless we have a delivery." Molly glanced at Stephanie. "I locked the front door when I left."

"Did Ana Jordan come in here last night?"

"I didn't see her."

"Did you see her at all yesterday?"

Molly exchanged a quick look with Stephanie. "Er . . . yesterday," she said at last. "I . . . er . . . spoke to her outside the shop."

"And you didn't see her again before you left last night?"

"No, I didn't. That reminds me." She opened her purse and took out a key. Handing it to Stephanie she said, "Now that I'm back on the morning shift, you'll need this back."

Stephanie took the key and held it out to Clara. "You'll need this to lock up at night. We really should get another one cut."

"If you don't mind," Dan said, "I'm not done asking Molly questions."

Molly looked guilty. "Oh, sorry."

"Where did you go when you left here?"

Again she paused before answering. "Home, of course. I was starving."

Clara curled her fingers into her palms. The voice had come from nowhere, as it always did. Faint, like a whisper, and hard to understand. Before the words became clear, she deliberately shut the voice down in her mind, focusing instead on Dan's next words.

"Stephanie, you notice anything different when you came in this morning?"

Stephanie shook her head. "No, nothing. In fact, Clara and I were saying how nice everything looked." She glanced at Molly. "You did a great job of cleaning up."

"Can anyone — ?" Dan broke off as a loud rattling of the door handle made them all turn their heads. He muttered something and unlocked the door to reveal a frail-looking man with gray hair and glasses.

Dr. Harold Weinberg had been the Quinn

34

family's doctor since before Clara was born, and now served as the medical examiner for the small town. He nodded at her as he stepped into the store. "Good to see you back in town, Clara. I heard it was for good this time."

"I hope so." Clara caught Stephanie's sharp look and smiled at her.

"About time, Hal." The chief clapped a hand on the other man's shoulder. "They're waiting for us back there." He looked at all three women in turn. "Don't anyone leave. I'm not done yet." Giving the doctor a hefty nudge, he followed him down the aisle to the stockroom.

Molly let out her breath in a rush of air. "What is it about talking to a policeman that always makes you feel guilty?" She uttered a shaky laugh. "I broke out in a sweat talking to Dan. Now I need to go home and take another shower."

"Well, you can't leave yet." Stephanie shot a nervous glance down the aisles. "Dan told us to stay here."

"I was kidding." Sounding more like herself, Molly leaned across the counter and squeezed Stephanie's hand. "Don't worry, Steph. You had nothing to do with all this. The cops will find out who did it, and then it will be all over. Look on the bright side.

You won't have to worry about Ana Jordan anymore."

Stephanie gasped. "Molly! That's a terrible thing to say! The poor woman is lying dead in our stockroom. How can you be so callous?"

Molly shrugged. "I'm sorry she's dead, but no one liked her. I don't know anyone who'll shed any tears over her, except maybe Frannie. I guess she'll be out of a job now. Unless whoever takes over the store keeps her on."

"What I want to know," Stephanie said, hugging herself again, "is why *was* Ana in our stockroom? How did she get in there? I have the only key to the back door, and there are only two keys to the front door. Mine and the one I gave you."

"Don't ask me." Molly wandered over to the door and peered through the glass pane. "There's a little crowd forming outside."

Stephanie glanced at the clock. "Oh, crap. Look at the time. Our customers are starting to arrive. What are we going to tell them?"

"The truth, I guess." Clara opened one of the books and stood it on top of the pile. "We can't tell them anything anyway until Dan unlocks the door."

"She's right." Molly marched back to the

36

counter. "They will just have to wait until he's done back there."

"All I hope," Stephanie said, "is that they find out who did this and soon. I don't like the idea of a murderer hanging out in Finn's Harbor."

Molly shuddered. "Just the word murderer sends cold shivers down my spine."

"Me, too." Stephanie started as the door to the stockroom banged open, and they heard the squeaky wheels of the gurney.

Clara turned away from the sight of the mound under the white sheet. She hadn't much liked Ana Jordan, either, but no one deserved to end her days in such a brutal way.

The medics caused a sensation among the small huddle of customers outside, but they refused to answer any questions.

Dan appeared a few minutes later, followed by Tim, and seemed in a hurry. "I'm gonna have to close you down for the day," he said, as he paused at the door. "I'll post a notice outside for your customers."

Stephanie uttered a cry of dismay. "What about those people out there?"

"I'll speak to them." As the two stepped outside, a chorus of voices demanded an explanation, and Dan delivered a short speech about the death of Ana Jordan, then pinned a notice on the door before leaving.

"What do we do now?"

Stephanie looked bewildered, and Clara put an arm about her shoulders. "We've got everything set up for the sale, so why don't we all go home? You both need a rest after the long day you had yesterday. Tomorrow we'll come back and finish up the sale."

"What about them?" Stephanie nodded her head at the small group of people out on the sidewalk. "They don't look as if they're ready to go home."

"Once they see that we've left, they'll leave as well." Clara picked up her purse and hung it over her shoulder, then led the way out the door.

Outside people were talking about the murder, speculating on who had hated Ana enough to want her dead. Clara caught sight of a woman huddled against the wall as if she were afraid to move away from it. Her face was white and tear-stained, and she kept pushing stringy, graying hair out of her eyes.

Recognizing Francis Dearly, one of Ana's employees, Clara realized that this woman was the only person who had shown any sorrow over Ana Jordan's death.

Stephanie must have seen her, too. She hurried over to her and beckoned Clara to follow. "Frannie, you remember Clara, don't you?" she said, as her cousin reached them.

The woman nodded at her. "You probably don't remember me, but I used to babysit you two when you were little."

A flash of memory gave Clara a vague vision of a painfully thin teenager with straggly brown hair and glasses. "Of course I remember you. It's good to see you again, though I wish it were under better circumstances."

The woman's face crumpled, and Stephanie awkwardly patted her shoulder. "I'm so sorry, Frannie. It must have been a dreadful shock for you."

Frannie nodded, then fished several tissues out of her pants pocket and blew her nose. "Please excuse me. I just can't believe it. I was just talking to her last night, and now . . ." She drew a shuddering breath. "Now she's *gone!*"

Her last word was delivered on a wail, and Clara said quickly, "We know how you feel. It was a shock to us, too."

"What about the store?" Stephanie nodded at the entrance to Jordan's Stationer's, where people hovered uneasily, talking to each other in low whispers.

"It's locked up." Frannie sniffed. "That's when I first knew something was wrong.

Ana always gets here early to open up, and when I found the door locked I knew something must have happened to her." She started crying again. "I never imagined it would be this."

"Well, I think you should go home." Stephanie looked around. "Did you ride your bike to work?"

Frannie nodded and blew her nose on a wad of tissues.

"I can give you a ride home," Clara offered. "My car is down the hill in the parking lot."

"Thank you, but I'd rather bike home. The fresh air will help clear my head."

She tried to smile, failed, and walked off quickly, the tissues clamped firmly to her nose.

"I feel so sorry for her," Stephanie said, as she watched the frail woman turn the corner of the building. "She's worked here forever. I wonder what she'll do now?"

"I guess that depends on what happens with the store." Clara looked past her cousin's shoulder at the few people left outside the bookstore. "Where did Molly go?"

"She took off." Stephanie sighed. "The last I saw of her she was running down the street thumbing numbers into her cell phone. I've forgotten how it feels to be that young and have a life."

"I should think with a husband and three young kids you have plenty of life."

"You know what I mean." Stephanie returned a wave as the last of the spectators walked away. "A life with dates and boyfriends and an exciting future just around the corner. Sometimes I miss that."

Clara's stomach churned. "If you ask me, we've had more than enough excitement for one day."

"That's different. Don't remind me. I'm trying to put it out of my mind for a while." Stephanie heaved a long sigh. "What about you? Won't you miss your exciting life in New York? It must be hard coming back to a sleepy little town like Finn's Harbor."

Clara avoided looking at her. "It's home. Besides, New York isn't nearly as exciting as you might think." She glanced across the street. "There's that guy again."

Stephanie turned her head to look. "What guy?"

"The guy across the street." Clara jerked her head. "There, outside the hardware store."

"Oh, that's Rick." Stephanie turned back and studied her cousin. "Rick Sanders. He's the new owner of Parson's Hardware. Fairly

41

new, anyway. Come to think about it, he's been there a few months now. I wonder when he's going to change the name of the store."

Clara watched the man dump a barrel full of brooms, rakes and shovels outside the store. "He's got muscle power; I'll give him that."

"Clara Quinn! Are you interested? He's single you know, and he's certainly tall enough for you. Good looking, too."

Clara scowled at her cousin. "No, I'm not interested. I'm done with men for good."

Stephanie looked taken aback. "For good? You're never going to get married and have kids?"

"Not if I can help it." Clara decided it was a good time to change the subject. "By the way, I'm only five ten, so you can quit the tall cracks."

Stephanie looked repentant. "Sorry, but I've spent my entire life literally looking up at you. Seven inches difference between us is hard to ignore. Remember how we got teased in high school? They called us Lofty and Shorty."

Clara pulled a face. "How can I forget? You keep reminding me."

"Sorry again." Stephanie jumped as her cell phone sang out its annoying little tune.

She answered it, frowning, spoke briefly, then snapped it shut and dropped it in her purse with a resigned expression on her face. "That was my mom. She heard about the murder and she's freaking out."

Clara felt a twinge of uneasiness. "My mom's probably heard about it by now, too. I imagine the whole town knows. We'd better get home." She had about three hours before her mother would be home from her job at the local library. She wasn't looking forward to having to recount the whole horrible experience. She needed those hours to be alone and get herself together again.

She set off, with Stephanie on her heels, and together they made their way to the parking lot, where they parted company.

After she let herself into the house, Clara rushed straight to her room and closed the door. She wanted to throw herself on the bed and bury her head under a pillow, but she resisted the urge. She had e-mails to write to the few people she wanted to keep in touch with in New York. It would help keep her mind off the horrible events of the morning.

It was an hour or so later when Stephanie called. The minute she began to speak, Clara could tell she was upset. "You're not going to believe this," Stephanie said, sounding angry and tearful. "Those idiots at the police station are holding Molly for questioning in Ana's murder."

"What?" For an instant Clara remembered the soft voice trying to tell her something when Molly was talking. Impatiently brushing the memory aside, she asked sharply, "Have they charged her?"

"Not yet. She asked Tim Rossi — the officer with Dan this morning — to let me know she might not be at work tomorrow." Stephanie sounded close to tears. "Oh, Clara, I know Molly didn't kill Ana. I just know it. We've got to help her."

Clara blinked. "Us? How can we help her? We're not lawyers."

"We have to find out who did kill Ana. Until we do, everyone will think Molly did it. Even if the cops can't prove it. It will destroy her."

Clara gripped the phone, praying that Stephanie didn't mean what she thought she meant. "Just how are we going to do that?"

The dreaded words echoed in her ear like the sound of doom.

"You can do it, Clara. You have to use the Quinn Sense and find out who killed Ana Jordan."

3

"You've got to be kidding!" Clara struggled to keep her tone calm. "Stephanie, I don't have any control over the Quinn Sense. It comes and goes, and I never know when it's going to pop up, and even when it does, most of the time I have no idea what it's trying to tell me. It's never there when I need it, and it's totally, utterly unreliable."

She must have sounded more adamant than she'd intended, as there was a long pause on the other end of the line. Finally, Stephanie's voice mumbled in her ear. "I know you hate it, and I'll never understand why, but we have to do something to help Molly, and you're the only one —"

"Molly will be fine. If she's innocent, then Dan will know it, and she'll be home any time now. He's just trying to find out as much as he can."

"Then why did he have her brought to the station? Why didn't he just question her at the bookstore when he was there?"

Clara hesitated. "Maybe he thought she'd tell him more if she felt intimidated."

"Like what?" Stephanie paused, then added, "You think she did it, don't you?"

Closing her eyes, Clara remembered Molly's fierce voice. *If you won't do anything, then I will.* "No, of course not —"

"Well, I know she didn't, and I'll find some way to help her. I have to go now. I'll see you at the store tomorrow."

Clara winced as the line went dead. Her cousin's accusing voice still rung in her ears. Sighing, she replaced the receiver. It wasn't as if she didn't want to help Molly, but Stephanie was expecting too much if she thought the Quinn Sense was going to solve the case.

For one thing, she'd spent too many years trying to shut the annoying voices down forever. It must have worked. The one time she'd desperately needed the Sense it had let her down. She suspected that the Quinn family's unusual talents were like muscles. The less you used them, the less effective they were.

She was about to return to her e-mails when she heard the front door snap shut. A couple of minutes later, her mother flung open the bedroom door without knocking, her eyes wide and disbelieving. "Is it true?"

Clara bit back the hasty words forming in her mind. Her mother still treated her like a schoolkid, and one of these days, she'd have a conversation about respecting privacy. Right now, though, there was a more important issue to talk about. "Yes," she said quietly. "It's true. Someone killed Ana Jordan in the stockroom of Stephanie's bookstore."

Her mother's gasp of horror seemed to echo around the room. "That poor child! How did she take it?" She rushed into the room and flung herself down on the bed. "She must be absolutely devastated!"

"She's kind of shook up, yes." Clara regarded her mother with an air of resignation. Jessica Quinn had always looked and dressed younger than her years. Now that she'd had her short hair colored and added false eyelashes, she could easily pass for a woman in her early forties instead of fifty-five.

If she didn't know better, Clara might have suspected that her mother was looking to replace her dead husband. In spite of the glamorous image, though, Clara knew Jessie was still grieving. They both were, and her mother's new look was simply a defense against the pain that still lingered after more than two years.

"By the way," she said, with just a hint of reproach, "I was a little upset, too, since I was the one who found her."

"Oh, yes, I did hear that." Jessie looked repentant. "How are you doing?"

"I'm okay." Clara looked at her watch. "You're home early."

"I left early." Jessie got up from the bed and smoothed her skirt over her slim hips. "As soon as I heard the news, I felt I had to get home and find out what happened. I'm going to make some tea, so let's go into the kitchen and you can fill me in on all the details."

Clara sent a reluctant glance at her laptop, then closed the lid. She wouldn't get any peace until she'd told her mother everything she knew, so she might as well get it over with, and maybe she'd still have enough energy left over to finish her e-mails.

Across town, Stephanie set up the ironing board in her kitchen, grabbed a shirt from the basket, and started slapping the iron back and forth so hard it shot out a cloud of steam in protest.

She still couldn't believe that Clara had refused to help clear Molly's name. Her cousin had never refused her anything before. She'd only had to ask, and Clara had been there, ready and willing to take whatever risks were involved.

Stephanie slammed the iron down on the collar of the shirt. Clara had changed, that much was obvious. That crack about being done with men, for instance. Clara had mentioned a boyfriend more than once but had refused to go into details. Not like the old days when they'd shared every thought and dream. The longer Clara had stayed in New York, the more secretive and reserved she'd become. Unlike her cousin — blurting out everything as it came to mind.

She'd been so looking forward to Clara coming back to Finn's Harbor to live. She'd envisioned the two of them just as they'd been in the past — eager daredevils ready to take on the world. Sure, she was married now and had three kids to take care of, and she was happy being a wife and mother, but deep down she was still Steffie, looking for excitement around every corner.

Stephanie let out a wistful sigh. It had been a long time since Clara had called her Steffie. It had been a very long time since she and Clara had exchanged secrets.

She shook out the shirt and hung it on a hanger, giving it a gentle pat before reaching in the laundry basket for another shirt to iron. Not that she'd trade her life with George and the kids for any kind of adventure.

Still, there was no one else she could share her deepest, most intimate hopes and fears with the way she had with Clara, and she missed that. She missed it a lot.

A forlorn tear splashed onto her fingers, and she jabbed an impatient hand at her cheek. Lifting the iron, she flattened a sleeve and was about to tackle it when the soft click of a closing door froze her hand.

Her quick glance at the clock confirmed that it was way too early for her mother to be bringing the kids home. George never got home before dinnertime, and it was still only the middle of the afternoon.

Someone was in the house.

Her thoughts flew to the still form underneath the sheet on the gurney. Clara hadn't let her near the stockroom after she'd found Ana's body, but Stephanie's imagination filled in a pretty good picture. *What if she were next?*

Her heart pounded so hard it shook her entire body. She grabbed hold of the iron, pulled out the plug, then crept over to the fridge. If the person who entered her house came into the kitchen, he was going to get a nasty headache.

Ears straining and arm raised, she waited. Maybe she'd imagined the door closing. Her arm ached, and she lowered the iron. Perhaps she should just take a look.

She took a step forward then froze again. *That creak.* She knew it well. It was the third stair from the top. She'd caught her kids sneaking downstairs more than once because of it. *He was going up to the bedrooms.*

Holding her breath, she edged toward the counter where she'd left her cell phone. She had to put the iron down to open the phone, and she quickly jabbed 911 with her thumb.

Patty, the dispatcher, sounded awfully loud when she answered. "Finn's Harbor Police. What's your emergency?"

"There's someone in my house," Stephanie whispered. "Please hurry."

"Address?"

Stephanie whispered it, almost choking on her dry throat. "Please, hurry up. It could be the murderer."

"Stephanie? Is that you?"

"Yes."

"Please try to stay calm. I'm sending Dan over right away. Where is the intruder?"

"Upstairs." Stephanie sent a fearful look at the entrance to the kitchen. "Please hurry!"

"Can you lock yourself in the bathroom?"

There were two ways out of the kitchen. One led to the dining room. The other into the living room. The hallway and the stairs were just beyond. To get to the downstairs bathroom she'd have to cross the living room in full view of the stairs. "No."

"The back door? Can you get out that way?"

Again she'd have to cross in front of the stairs. How much time would she have before he was flying down them to reach her?

Her legs trembled at the thought. "No, I . . ." She broke off with a gasp. "He's coming down. Please *hurry!*"

She shoved the phone in her pocket and grabbed the iron again. Okay, it was up to her now. Praying Dan would get there in time, she tiptoed over to the fridge again.

The iron was heavy, and her hand shook, rattling the water inside it. He'd hear it the moment he came into the kitchen. She tried to steady her hand and prayed for the strength to hit him hard enough.

He was almost at the kitchen. She could hear his footsteps on the hardwood floor. Raising the iron, she got ready to strike.

"Steph? Stephanie? Where are you?"

With a cry she dropped the iron. It crashed

to the floor inches from her foot, but she didn't even notice. She was too busy wrapping her arms around the neck of her surprised husband.

"George! What are you doing home? I thought . . . I thought . . ." She gulped, then burst into noisy tears.

George gathered her in his arms, and it felt so comforting she managed to calm her sobs to loud sniffles. "I got off early," he said, nuzzling her ear. "I thought you might be feeling a bit shaky after what happened this morning, so I asked for the time off."

"Why didn't you call me?" She sniffed and wiped her nose on her sleeve.

"I figured you'd be lying down since the kids aren't here. I didn't want to disturb you."

She sniffed again, and pulled out of his arms to find a box of tissues. "I thought you were the killer coming after me."

"Oh, honey, I'm sorry —" He broke off and raised his head. "What's that?"

Stephanie's stomach took a nosedive. "What?" A sudden screeching of tires turned her head toward the window.

"That," George said, and headed out of the kitchen.

A car door slammed, and Stephanie heard George open the front door. Then she remembered. "Oh, crap," she muttered, and hurried out after him just in time to see Dan charging up the driveway, with Tim right behind him.

Dan pulled up when he saw George, then looked at Stephanie.

"So, where's the intruder?"

George looked down at her, frowning. "Intruder?"

Stephanie sighed. "Come on in, Dan, and I'll explain." Feeling like a complete idiot, she led them into the kitchen.

"I guess George had a lucky escape," Dan said, when she finished telling him what happened. He looked across the table at George. "You might wanna wear a hard hat when you come home in future." There wasn't so much as a glimmer of a smile on his face, though Tim looked as if he was struggling not to laugh.

Stephanie puffed out her breath. "Okay, so I overreacted. But I was scared. I had a dead body lying in my stockroom this morning. That's enough to put anyone's nerves on edge. By the way, while we're on the subject, why on earth would you think that Molly had anything to do with it? You know very well she couldn't have killed Ana."

Dan pinched his lips together, and Tim

shot him an uneasy glance. "No," Dan said, in his slow drawl, "I really don't know that."

"There was no sign of a break-in," Tim put in, "and Molly was the last one in the shop and the only one with a key. She —"

He broke off as Dan gave him a scathing look.

"I have a key, too." Stephanie glared at Dan. "Does that make me a suspect?"

"You left the store at three. Doc Weinberg says that Ana Jordan died sometime between nine and eleven."

"I could have gone back."

"But you didn't," George said, sounding anxious. "You were here with me and the kids. Why are you trying to incriminate yourself?"

"I'm just trying to show that it could have been someone else other than Molly." Stephanie turned back to Dan. "What if someone came into the stockroom and hid in there until Molly left?"

George answered her before Dan could speak. "That doesn't explain why Ana was in there."

"Maybe he lured her in there. It could happen."

Dan sighed. "Anything's possible, and we're considering all the options. I'm not saying that Molly meant to kill Ana, but if she did, accident or not, she's going to answer for it. She's scared right now, and I can understand that. Sooner or later, if she's guilty, she'll own up to it."

"And what if she's not?" Stephanie glared at him. "What if someone did intend to kill Ana, and we have a dangerous murderer running around? What about fingerprints? Did you look for those?"

George laid a hand on her arm. "Honey . . ."

She ignored him. "There must be fingerprints somewhere in there."

"We found plenty. All smudged. Nothing we could use." Dan nodded at George. "Don't worry; we'll get to the truth eventually. We always do." He got up from the table and gestured to Tim with a jerk of his thumb. "Now we'd best be getting back to the station. Meanwhile, I suggest you stop worrying about it and leave the police business to us." He nodded at George. "Glad everything's okay here."

"Thanks for coming." George followed him out of the kitchen. "Sorry for the false alarm."

Dan said something Stephanie didn't catch, but she did hear Tim laugh as they went out the door. Scowling, she went back to the ironing board. They might be laughing at her right now, but if Finn's Harbor's killer struck again, that would wipe the silly smiles right off their faces.

If there was one thing she was certain of, it was that Molly didn't kill Ana Jordan. That meant that someone else did, and until he was found, they were all in danger.

"What I don't understand," Jessie Quinn said, placing a glass of iced tea on the kitchen table in front of Clara, "is how Ana got into the stockroom without Molly seeing her or the killer. It just doesn't make sense."

"No, it doesn't." Clara picked up the glass. "None of it makes sense."

"Do you think Molly was lying?"

"I don't know." Clara sipped her tea. "I don't know Molly well enough to tell. The important thing is that Stephanie believes Molly's telling the truth."

Jessie shook her head. "Why was Ana in the bookstore in the first place? I'd heard she'd sworn never to set foot in there. She called it a den of iniquity, or something like that." She sat down at the table and took a sip from her glass. "Makes the Raven's Nest sound like a stripper club or something."

Clara smiled. "It's hardly that. Stephanie said that Ana was afraid the occult books would turn children into demons."

Jessie snorted. "Just the kind of thing she would say. We shouldn't speak ill of the dead, but that woman could poison the mind of a saint. No wonder nobody liked her."

"That's sad." Clara wiped the condensation from the side of her glass with her thumb. "She must have been a very unhappy person."

"Unhappy, perhaps, but that doesn't excuse some of the spiteful things she's done." Jessie put down her glass, rattling the ice inside. "Look at what she did to poor John Halloran. Just about ruined his whole life."

Clara frowned. "John Halloran? Isn't he the guy who owned the candy store?"

"Yes, the Sweet Spot, right down the street from Jordan's. It's the Pizza Parlor now."

Clara nodded. "Oh, that's right. Stephanie and I went there the last time I was home. We met the new owner. Tony something."

"Manetas. He's Greek." Jessie laughed and lifted a hand to fluff her hair. "Very good looking for his age, and quite the lady's man, if you want my opinion."

Clara eyed her mother's flushed cheeks with interest. Maybe the mourning period was over after all. "So what did Ana do to John Halloran to ruin his life?"

"Ah, yes." Jessie reached for her glass again. "Well, when John first opened that store, he sold mostly candy. He and Ana were great pals back then. I remember when her father was in the hospital, John used to close up Jordan's for her so she could visit the old man."

"So what happened?"

"Well, John decided to expand a little. He started with Christmas decorations, then got into gift wrap and greeting cards."

"I remember. He sold those really cute cards designed by a local artist."

"Yes, well, apparently, those greeting cards were so popular they were cutting into Ana's sales. She started spreading rumors about John, hinting that he was a child molester or something. His business went down like a popped balloon. He sold the shop, his wife divorced him and took the kids to California. He never sees them. It's really sad."

"But surely people who knew him didn't believe the rumors? His wife must have known it was all lies?"

Jessie shrugged. "You know what they say, where there's smoke . . ."

Clara stared at her. "*You* believed it?"

"At first I did." Jessie twisted the glass in

her hands. "Then Frannie went to work for Ana, and she found out that John lost his business because of Ana's lies. The word soon got out."

"I wonder how Frannie learned about that. I doubt Ana confessed."

"Who knows? The important thing was that John could hold up his head again in Finn's Harbor. Though it was too late to save his business."

"Or his marriage, apparently."

"Yes, well, that was on shaky ground anyway from what John told me."

Clara shook her head. "What a terrible thing to do to someone. Why didn't he sue Ana for libel?"

Jessie shrugged. "Maybe he'd had enough of all the finger-pointing and didn't want to bring it up again. Or maybe he simply couldn't prove it. I guess something like that would be hard to prove. Whatever. It looks as if the hand of justice stepped in for him now, though, doesn't it?"

Clara didn't answer. She was seeing again the vision of Ana Jordan lying in a pool of blood. The hand of justice, or was it John Halloran's hand that had finally gotten even?

"Not a very good start to your new job, I'm afraid." Jessie lifted her glass again. "I can't believe something like this would happen in our sleepy little town. Once word of this gets out, it will kill the tourist trade. Not that I'd mind, of course. Tourists can be such a headache, cluttering up the sidewalks and littering the beaches. Not to mention the cars tearing down our streets."

"The tourists help to keep this town alive," Clara reminded her. "Without them, I don't know if anyone would stay in business."

"Well, Stephanie seems to be doing well, I'm happy to say." Jessie gave her a speculative look. "She's fortunate you decided to come back here to live. She must be thrilled you're helping her out in the bookstore."

"She knows it's only temporary, until she finds someone permanent."

"I still don't know why you left New York. I thought you were doing so well there." Jessie reached for the jug and refilled her glass. "This is such a dinky little town. It must seem like the back of beyond after living in the Big Apple."

"It's peaceful here." Clara pushed her chair back and picked up her empty glass. "At least, it was, until this morning."

"Clara, when are you going to tell me why you really left New York?"

Clara paused, nerves tightening all the way

down her back.

"I already told you. I got tired of all the hassles. I missed home. I missed my family. I'd had enough of big-city life."

"I know what you told me." Jessie got up and carried her glass and the jug over to the counter. "I just can't help thinking there's a lot you're not telling me."

Clara walked over to join her at the sink. "Quit worrying, Mom. I'm not a kid anymore. I'm a grown woman. I know what I'm doing, and right now I'm doing what I want to do. I'm happy to be home. Can't we just leave it at that?"

Jessie looked disappointed, but she put down the jug and patted Clara's arm. "Oh, very well. I suppose you'll tell me eventually. As a matter of fact, I never did understand why you left here in the first place. One of these days you'll have to satisfy my curiosity on that, too."

That, Clara thought, as she opened the dishwasher, was never going to happen. No one would ever know that she'd inherited the Quinn Sense. No one except Stephanie, anyway. And even Stephanie didn't know the real reason she'd left New York. That was something else she intended to keep to herself.

Shutting down the painful memories, she

placed the glass on the rack and closed the dishwasher.

4

Clara arrived at the Raven's Nest shortly before noon the next day. The yellow tape and the notice had been taken down, and the store seemed crowded with teens and parents taking advantage of the back-to-school sale.

Clara was relieved to see Molly standing behind the counter, ringing up a purchase for a couple of young customers. She looked up without her usual smile as Clara approached. "Steph's in the back," she said, jerking her head in that direction. "Talking to Mrs. Riley." She handed the bag of books over to the giggling girls and waited for them to leave before adding, "She didn't want me helping her. Can you believe that?"

Clara raised her eyebrows. "Stephanie?"

Molly rolled her eyes. "No, Mrs. Riley. She said she'd feel more comfortable if Steph found her a book. I guess she thinks I killed Ana, and now she's afraid of me."

"That's nonsense." Clara walked behind the counter and stashed her purse on a shelf. "Dan would never have let you go if he thought you were a murderer."

"That's just it." Molly turned mournful green eyes on her. "He does think I did it. He just can't prove it."

"Did he say that?"

Molly picked up a stack of bookmarks and started loading them into a wooden holder. "Someone told him I threatened Ana that morning."

"Yes, but —"

"He said that I was the last one to leave the store and the only one with a key. There was no sign of a break-in. He thinks Ana was mad at Stephanie and came into the store meaning to cause damage or something and that I tried to stop her."

"That's ridiculous."

"It's what everyone else is thinking, too. The whole town believes I murdered Ana."

"Of course they don't." Clara put an arm about Molly's shoulders and gave her a hug. "We know you didn't do it, and anyone who knows you will know it, too."

"A lot of people heard me yelling at her yesterday."

"That doesn't mean you killed her."

Molly's eyes filled with tears. "I didn't like

her, Clara, but I'd never want her dead. I didn't kill her, I swear it."

The words seemed to fill Clara's mind, swirling around and settling down like snowflakes tossed by the wind. The voice in her head whispered, soft and insistent. She shut it down, refusing to listen. "I know you didn't," she said, squeezing Molly's shoulders again before letting her go. "And so will everyone else."

As if to contradict her, Mrs. Riley's voice rang out loud and clear as she walked up the aisle with Stephanie. "I'm not giving my credit card to that young woman. I just don't trust her."

"I'll see to it," Stephanie said, and hurried up to the counter. "Molly, would you please stock the cookbook shelves for me? There's some boxes that came in last week. I left them under the table over there."

Molly gave Clara a look that clearly said, *I told you so,* and hurried off.

Clara smiled at the elderly woman as she reached the counter. "I'll take that for you," she said, holding out her hand.

The woman scowled at her. "Who are you?"

"This is my cousin, Clara Quinn." Stephanie hurried around the counter. "You must remember her. She went to New York to live, but she's back now." She looked at Clara. "You remember Mrs. Riley, don't you?"

Clara exchanged a meaningful glance with her. She remembered the woman all right. The town gossip. If you wanted to dig up dirt on people in town, you asked Mrs. Riley. "Of course," she said, still smiling. "It's nice to see you again, Mrs. Riley."

"Do I know you?" Mrs. Riley peered closer. "Oh, yes, now I see. You look older." She ran a critical glance over Clara. "Lost weight, too. You must have been starving in New York City."

Clara held on to her smile. "May I take your card?"

Mrs. Riley handed over her card, and Clara rang up the purchase. After slipping the book into a bag, she held it out to the impatient woman.

Mrs. Riley practically snatched it out of her hand. "Thank you, and if you want my advice, you'll get rid of that nasty-tempered witch before she does something dreadful to someone else." She marched off, sticking her nose in the air as she passed Molly on her way out.

"What did I tell you?" Stephanie demanded, her voice low and fierce. "Everyone thinks Molly killed Ana. We have to find out who really did it. Dan's convinced it was Molly; he's not even going to look for anyone else. She *needs* us, Clara! She needs the Quinn Sense!"

Clara winced. This was exactly what she'd been afraid of — being forced to deal with the dratted curse again. All her life she'd been unable to say no to her cousin, even when she knew it would end badly. This time certainly seemed to be no exception.

Stephanie's pleading eyes, however, were impossible to ignore. "All right. We'll look into it, though I don't know what we can do that Dan can't. You do know that messing in police business, especially murder, can get us in a whole lot of trouble?"

Stephanie's smile wavered on her face. "It wouldn't be the first time."

"Maybe not," Clara said grimly, "but this could be real trouble. The kind where you get hurt. Or worse."

Stephanie looked across the room to where Molly stood, head down, her face hidden by her hair. "If it will help to clear Molly's name, it'll be worth the risk."

"What about George? What will he say when he finds out you're hunting down a killer?"

Stephanie shrugged. "I'll tell George what he needs to know. Besides, you'll have to do most of the legwork. I see myself as more on the idea side of things.

"Gee, thanks." Clara twisted her mouth in a wry smile. "Just like old times."

"Yeah, just like old times." Stephanie put an arm around her cousin. "You used to be so good at using the Sense. Do you remember when you told me that George was going to dump Ana for me?"

Clara sighed. "I remember. You refused to believe me and actually accused me of trying to stir up trouble between you and George."

"I know." Stephanie rubbed her fingers across her forehead. "It just seemed so utterly impossible. George had never spoken a word to me. He was a huge basketball star, and in those days Ana was a real hottie. She knew all the tricks and I knew nothing."

"Ah, but the voices were telling me that George was getting tired of Ana's antics and had his eye on you. It was just a matter of time before he made his move."

Stephanie clasped her hands in front of her throat. "And he did. The Quinn Sense never lies."

"No, it just disappears when you need it the most."

Stephanie's smile faded. "You'll get it all back. I know it."

Clara sincerely hoped not. "You're determined to do this, then."

"With or without you. I just hope it's with you. You know, two heads and all that."

"I'll help on one condition."

"What's that?"

Clara turned back to the counter. "At the first sign of real danger, we call Dan."

"Agreed."

"And no more talk about the Quinn Sense."

"But —"

Clara held up her hand. "No buts. Now let's go tell Molly we're going to try and clear her name."

Tears welled in Molly's eyes when Stephanie told her they wanted to find the killer. "I'll help," she told them, hugging each of them in turn. "Just tell me what to do."

"Well, nothing for the moment," Stephanie said, as the bell jangled on the door, signaling another customer. "But as soon as we get a break, we'll sit down and discuss our strategy. Right now, though, someone has to clean up the mess in the stockroom. No one's set foot in there since the police were here, and we need to get the new stock on the shelves."

Molly's face lost its color, and she swallowed. "I'll do it. I may puke, though."

Clara took a deep breath. "I'll help. It won't be so bad if we both do it."

Molly sent her a grateful look. "You two are the best friends anyone could ask for, and I hope you know how much this means to me."

"We're doing what's right," Stephanie said, patting her on the shoulder. "We know you didn't kill Ana, and that means someone else did. He's not going to get away with it. We might not be able to arrest him or anything, but maybe if we find out enough about what happened, we can help Dan to go after him."

Molly twitched her eyebrows. "I just don't know what you can really do if Dan wasn't able to find anything."

"Exactly," Clara murmured.

Stephanie ignored her. "People are more likely to talk to us than Dan. Most people are afraid to say too much to the police, in case it gets them into trouble."

Molly nodded, her face brightening just a little. "You're right. Besides, you can do things and go places the police can't go without a warrant or something." She jerked a thumb over her shoulder. "Okay, Clara. Let's go tackle that stockroom."

It was almost at the end of Molly's shift before things quieted down in the bookstore long enough for them all to sit down with a cup of coffee in the Reading Nook.

Stephanie settled back in the comfy armchair with a long sigh. "It's been a busy day. Everyone's heard about what happened to Ana, and they're coming in to satisfy their curiosity."

"I know." Clara leaned forward to straighten the magazines on the low table. "They all want to talk about the murder. They get miffed when I tell them I don't know any more than they do. Like I'm hiding something from them."

"They think you're protecting me," Molly said, staring down at her feet. "They're all avoiding me. I feel like a leper. One of the untouchables."

"Don't worry." Stephanie leaned forward to touch her arm. "We'll clear your name. Won't we, Clara?"

Clara caught her breath. "That reminds me, I might have a suspect."

"You do?"

"Who is it?"

They'd both spoken at once, and Clara looked over her shoulder to make sure they were alone. "John Halloran. Well, I guess he's not really a suspect, but he certainly had a motive. He had good reason to hate Ana."

Stephanie slumped her shoulders. "So did half the people in town."

"Ah, but half the people in town didn't lose a business and a marriage because of Ana's lies."

Molly sat up. "How did she manage to do all that?"

Clara repeated a shortened version of what her mother had told her.

"John's a regular customer here," Stephanie said. "He comes in all the time. I know he's a little weird, but he seems like such a quiet man — not at all the kind of person who would kill someone."

"Few people do." Clara stretched out her legs and wiggled her aching toes. "Everyone has his breaking point, though. John Halloran could have been harboring resentment all this time, and some little thing could easily have set him off."

"Like what?"

Clara shrugged. "I don't know. Something Ana said to him, or something he heard somewhere."

Stephanie considered that for a moment before answering. "Well, if that's so, he's not the only one. I know someone else who suffered because of Ana's lies."

Molly's eyes gleamed with hope. "Who?"

"Rick Sanders."

Clara stared at her. "The guy across the street?"

"Yep. He used to work for Ana's father, Henry. That was before this store existed. This used to be part of Jordan's Stationer's, remember?"

"Of course I do. I remember when Ana sold off this part of the building after her father died."

Stephanie uttered a soft gasp. "Maybe that's how Ana got into the stockroom. If our two stores used to be all one building, and the locks were never changed, she could still have had keys to the Raven's Nest."

Clara sat up. "So could anyone who has worked for her."

Both women stared at her as if she'd just announced the end of the world.

"Oh, wow," Molly whispered.

Eyes gleaming, Stephanie nodded. "That does explain a few things. I remember George telling me that Ana's father had left her a load of debt and she had to sell the annex to help keep the store afloat."

"Well, I'm glad she did," Molly said, looking around. "I love the Raven's Nest, and so do most of the people in this town."

"But what about Rick Sanders?" Clara leaned forward. "What lies did Ana tell about him?"

"Well, according to George, who heard it from a couple of people, Ana fired Rick right after she took over the store. She more or less accused him of stealing from her father, which accounted for the bad debts. Rick swore he never took anything. He said she fired him because she was afraid he'd buy her out. Apparently, he had money from an inheritance, and he knew more about how that store was run than she did."

Molly gasped. "I can't believe that no one ever took that woman to court."

Stephanie shrugged. "Well, I guess there was no way to prove it. George said that Ana was clever and never actually came right out and said anything specific. She just sort of hinted, and people took it from there. Anyway, it was her word against Rick's, and Ana grew up in Finn's Harbor. Everyone knew her. Rick was the stranger in town."

"Well, it didn't stop him from eventually taking over his own store, right across the street," Molly said. "He's doing pretty well with it, too, from what I hear." She yawned and looked at her watch. "Only I don't see what any of this has to do with Ana's murder. Rick's a nice guy. He doesn't seem like a killer any more than John Halloran does."

"You can never tell what a person is really like unless you live with him." Clara was unable to keep the bitterness out of her voice. Meeting Stephanie's curious stare, she added quickly, "I guess there's a lot of people in town who had a reason to hate Ana Jordan, and that just makes it all the harder to figure out who killed her."

"We have to start asking questions," Stephanie said. "Like, who was on the street late Friday night and what were they doing there?"

"Motive and opportunity." Clara frowned. "What's the third thing?"

"Means!" Molly looked pleased with herself. "I read a lot of mysteries. It means the murder weapon."

"Good. I'm glad someone knows what she's doing. Only in this case, anyone could have had the means bit. It wouldn't have been that hard to lift the bust and hit Ana over the head with it."

Stephanie nodded her agreement. "It would help if we knew why or how Ana was in the stockroom in the first place."

"Good point. I guess it wouldn't be that hard to lure her in there. It seems that just about everyone knew she wanted to shut down the bookstore. All the murderer would have to do is tell Ana there was something in the stockroom that would help her do that, and she'd follow him right in." Clara turned her head as the bell jangled. "There's a customer. I'd better get back to the counter."

Molly got up from her chair. "Well, I'm going home." She looked down at Clara. "Sure you'll be okay here on your own? I mean, you're not nervous or anything?"

"I think I know enough to manage." Clara glanced at Stephanie. "I can always call my cousin if I'm not sure about anything, right?"

Stephanie didn't answer her. She was peering toward the front of the store, a strange expression on her face.

Molly turned her head to see what she was looking at and drew a sharp breath. "It's John Halloran," she said, in a low whisper. "Now's your chance to question our first suspect, Clara. Get what you can out of him."

Clara had a sudden urge to hide. "I have no idea what to ask him."

"Think fast." Stephanie gave her a little push. "Use your talents. You'll come up with something." She ducked her head, avoiding Clara's glare, and slipped past her. "I have to get home to my kids," she said, following Molly, who was headed for the door. "Call me if you have any problems."

Clara watched them leave, the sinking feeling in her stomach growing worse by the minute. She'd been abandoned, left alone in the store with a possible murderer.

Very slowly, she walked up to the counter, conscious of her heels clicking on the polished floorboards. John Halloran was nowhere to be seen, though she could hear shuffling footsteps at the lower end of one of the aisles. He was awfully near the stockroom. Was he waiting for a chance to slip inside there to make sure he'd left no incriminating evidence behind?

Scolding herself, she moved behind the counter. She was being ridiculous. Even if the killer had left some kind of evidence behind, Dan would surely have found it by now. Even so, she strained her ears, listening for the possible closing of the stockroom door.

"It's nice to see you again, Clara."

The soft voice spoke from just a yard or so away, making her jump so violently her teeth clicked. She'd been so intent on listening, staring down at the counter, she hadn't seen him emerge from the aisle.

"Oh! Mr. Halloran!" Her voice sounded squeaky, and she coughed. "It's nice to see you, too."

He walked toward her, carrying two books under his arm. "I heard that you were working for your cousin. How nice that the two of you can enjoy this together." He waved a hand at the aisles. "Stephanie has done a good job with the store. Very impressive."

Clara cleared her throat. "Thank you. I'll tell her you said that."

"Oh, please do." He turned his head to look up at the crystals, revealing a large bald patch in the center of his light brown hair. "Nice touch."

"We like them." She kept staring at the bald patch, wondering how on earth she was going to find out where he was and what he was doing on the night of the murder. She couldn't just come out and ask him.

He turned toward her, and she quickly forced a smile. "I see you've found a couple of books. Can I ring those up for you?"

"Sure." Instead of handing them to her, however, he stared at her through the lenses of his black-rimmed glasses. "It must have been quite a shock for you young ladies to find Ana Jordan's body like that."

Clara swallowed hard. "Yes, it was." She could feel the pulse in her throat throbbing and swallowed again. "Quite a shock."

"Not the sort of thing you imagined coming home to find."

"No, not at all."

"Do the police have any idea who did it?"

"I don't think so."

"Someone said Dan was questioning Molly."

Clara raised her chin. "Dan questioned a lot of people. Molly had nothing to do with it."

John Halloran smiled. "Of course she didn't." He moved closer to lay the books on the counter, bringing with him the too-sweet scent of his cologne. "I wonder who did, though. Why in here? Unless whoever killed her wanted the police to think it was one of you. After all, Ana wanted to shut down the store, didn't she? And we all know how good she was at getting her own way. Who else had such a strong reason to want her out of the way?"

Clara curled her fingers into her palm. "Plenty of people, from what I hear."

His eyes narrowed just a bit. "Yes, I don't suppose there'll be too many mourners at her funeral."

"I wouldn't know."

"Well, I'm sure Dan will find our killer soon enough. This is a small town. Not a lot of places to hide, right?"

His laugh sent chills down her spine. Quickly she scanned the purchase and swiped his card. After handing him the sales slip, she dropped the books into a bag and pushed it toward him. "Thank you, Mr. Halloran."

"Oh, please, call me John. Everyone does." He picked up the bag and tucked it under his arm. "Good day, Clara. I'll be seeing you soon."

It sounded more like a threat than a promise. She managed a weak smile, conscious of Molly's words pounding in her head. *Get what you can out of him.* It was a lot easier to say it than to do it.

He was almost at the door when she blurted out, "I don't suppose you happened to see anything the night Ana was murdered?"

He paused so long she dug a channel into her palms with her nails. Then he turned, his pale gray eyes gleaming behind the glasses. "See anything?"

"Unusual, I mean. Something that could help us find out who did this awful thing."

"If I had," John Halloran said in his soft voice, "I would have certainly told the police."

"Oh, of course." Clara nodded her head at him, and then couldn't seem to stop nodding. "I was only wondering, that's all."

"We're all wondering." He turned back to

the door and opened it. "All except the murderer, of course." He started chuckling as he went out the door, and it closed behind him.

Clara let out all the breath she'd been holding in one big gasp and propped her elbows on the counter. So much for this detective work. It was a lot harder than she'd thought.

At least she hadn't heard voices in her head while she was talking to him. Just for a moment she almost wished she had. She might have learned something useful. As far as she could tell, John Halloran hadn't actually lied, though now that she thought about it, he hadn't said much at all.

Stephanie and Molly would probably be disappointed in her, though she couldn't see what more she could have done, other than ask him outright if he'd killed Ana. Not that he was likely to admit it, of course, but the voices might have been able to tell her if he'd lied.

There she went again. Darn the Quinn Sense. It was nothing but trouble when it was there, and it was never there when she could use it. Her biggest fear about coming back to Finn's Harbor was that she'd get it back full strength, and thinking about it all the time didn't help.

Annoyed with herself, she charged out from behind the counter and headed for the Reading Nook. Maybe a spurt of cleaning up would help take her mind off things. If there was one thing she didn't need, it was the Quinn Sense coming back to haunt her.

5

Stephanie called just as Clara was putting away the coffee cups. "So? What did you find out about John Halloran?" she demanded, when Clara picked up the phone.

"Not much." Clara told her what she remembered of the conversation. "I tried to find out where he was on Friday night, but he wasn't too helpful."

"Maybe you didn't ask the right questions."

"I'm not a cop, Stephanie. There are some things I can't ask without seeming nosy, or just plain accusing."

"I suppose." There was a pause, then Stephanie added, "Well, did he act suspicious at all? Did he seem nervous when you asked questions?"

Clara thought about it. "He was kind of creepy," she said at last. "The truth is, he made *me* nervous. I can't say that's incriminating, though. He really didn't say anything specific."

"Crap. We'll have to think of another way to find out this stuff."

"That's what I was afraid you'd say."

"Come on, Clara. Where's your sense of adventure?"

"Ten years in New York. That's what happened to it."

She hadn't meant to sound so caustic, and Stephanie caught on right away. "What's that supposed to mean? What happened to you in New York, Clara? Why won't you tell me?"

Clara attempted a light laugh. "Nothing happened to me. I just grew up, that's all."

Stephanie was silent for so long Clara thought she'd hung up. Then she said in a small voice, "That's a shame, Clara. That's a real shame. I'll see you tomorrow."

Clara had the uneasy feeling that once more she'd let her cousin down, but before she could answer, Stephanie hung up.

Molly had Mondays off, and when Clara arrived at the Raven's Nest late the next morning, it was to find Stephanie red-faced, her arms full of books and her bangs sticking to her forehead.

"I just got a big delivery," she said, hoisting the heavy pile in her arms, "and I need

85

to get them in the stockroom and get the shelves restocked. We haven't put any new fantasy books out since . . . before Dan closed the store."

Clara held out her hands. "Here, I'll take them."

"No, you watch the counter. I'll be quicker. I know where everything goes."

She tore off, and shaking her head, Clara moved behind the counter and stashed her purse. There must have been a rush of customers that morning, as sales slips lay scattered on the shelf instead of filed away in the drawer, and a couple of plastic bags had drifted to the floor.

Clara bent over to pick them up, grunting as she straightened. She tucked the bags into the slot where they belonged and turned back to the counter, coming face-to-face with the amused gaze of the man from across the street.

Suspect number two. Clara sent a frantic glance down the aisle, but could see no sign of Stephanie. "Er . . . good morning. Can I help you?" She swiped back a chunk of her hair and tucked it behind her ear.

"Well, technically it's afternoon," Rick Sanders said, glancing at the grandfather clock. "But I guess if you haven't had lunch yet, it must feel like it's still morning."

She stared at him, trying to figure out if he meant anything by all that. "Yes," she said at last. "I suppose you're right."

He stuck out a hand. "Hi. I'm Rick Sanders. I own the hardware store across the street. You must be Stephanie's cousin."

His smile made her feel a little less defensive. She tentatively gave him her hand, and it was immediately swallowed up in his. His strong grasp hurt a little, but strangely, it was a pleasurable kind of pain. "Yes, I'm Clara Quinn."

"Home from New York."

"Yes, I am." She seemed to be saying yes a lot. She struggled to think of something halfway intelligent to say, but it was hard to think with her hand still clasped in his.

"It's a pleasure to meet you, Clara. Stephanie talks about you all the time."

Really. She would have to ask Stephanie what she'd told him. "I hope she wasn't too explicit," she said, then wished she hadn't said that. It sounded a bit racy.

Rick's eyes gleamed with amusement. "Don't worry. It was just general stuff."

He really did have nice eyes. Dark brown and soft, like a puppy's. Nice mouth, too, especially when he smiled. Thick dark hair, cut short. She wondered if he colored it, then dismissed the thought. Strong men didn't color their hair.

She curled her fingers as, without warning, the voices started whispering in her head. *Wait!* What was she doing? He was on their list of suspects. A very short list. Dragging her hand out of his grasp, she shut the voices down. She didn't want to hear what they had to say. She would far rather suspect John Halloran of murder than this man with the quiet voice and the pleasant smile.

"So, what's the verdict?"

Confused, she frowned at him. "Sorry?"

His grin widened. "Well, you've been sizing me up pretty good. I was just wondering if I passed the test."

Oh, help. She could feel the blood rushing to her cheeks.

"Oh, sorry. I was just wondering if we've met before. It's hard to keep track when I've only been here on short visits for the last ten years."

"I think I would have remembered if we'd met. I —" Rick Sanders turned his head as Stephanie's voice rang out behind him.

"Oh, hi, there."

Stephanie came forward, an odd expression on her face. She gave Clara a meaningful look that meant absolutely nothing to her, then turned to their customer. "I hope you found what you were looking for?"

He looked back at Clara. "I sure did."

Clara felt her cheeks growing warmer. She was reading far too much into a casual remark. What the heck was the matter with her? Hadn't she learned a hard enough lesson to be immune to this kind of phony charm? The man could have killed Ana Jordan and left her to die. She'd better remember that.

Rick laid a cookbook on the counter. "Never could resist a good recipe. This looks like it has some good ones." He tapped the cover. "Italian cooking at its best. What more could you ask for?"

"What, indeed," Clara murmured. She rang up the purchase, bagged his book and handed it to him. "I hope it meets your expectations."

"I'm sure it will. I know what I like, and I don't usually go far wrong." His smile faded, and the intense look in his eyes unsettled her. "By the way, I'm sorry about what happened in here. That must have been a terrible shock. Not a very good welcome back to our peaceful little town."

Stephanie answered for her, walking forward with a determined expression that alarmed Clara. "Yes, it was. Quite a shock for all of us. I can't imagine who would want to hurt Ana like that."

Rick's mouth set in a thin line, changing his entire face. "Well, not to speak ill of the dead, but I'd be lying if I said I'd miss Ana Jordan. She was not a good person by any means. Some might even say she got what she deserved." With that he lifted his hand, gave them both a farewell wave and strode out of the store.

Clara finally felt as if she could breathe again.

Stephanie joined her behind the counter and gave her a hard stare. "Well? Why weren't you asking him questions?"

"Like what?"

"Like finding out what he was doing on the night of the murder? You heard him. He hated Ana."

Clara threw her hands up in disgust. "Why don't I just come right out and ask him if he killed her?"

"You can't do that."

"Exactly."

Stephanie leaned her back against the counter and rubbed her forehead. "There has to be a way to get information without insulting people."

"I told you. We're not lawyers, cops or reporters. They're the only ones who can go around asking questions without someone telling them to mind their own business."

Stephanie pouted, drawing her brows together in an effort to think. "Wait! I have an idea."

"Oh, good. Do tell."

If Stephanie recognized the sarcasm, she gave no sign. "You have to go out with Rick."

Clara gasped. "I *what?*"

Stephanie beamed. "He likes you. I can tell! You have to go on a date with him, make sure he has a glass or two of wine so he's nice and relaxed and casually bring up the subject of Friday night. You don't even have to mention Ana. We just want to know if he has an alibi."

Clara leaned her face into her cousin's. "I am *not* going out with him. *You* go out with him."

"I can't. I'm married." Stephanie half closed her eyes. "Though if I weren't, I wouldn't mind —"

"Cut that out!" Clara pulled in a deep breath. "Let Molly go out with him."

"He's too old for Molly. He has to be at least thirty-five or so. You *have* to do it."

"I don't *have* to do anything."

"You promised to help find the murderer. How can we do that if you turn down the first opportunity to get some important information?"

"Listen, I questioned John Halloran, didn't I?"

"And found out exactly nothing."

"That wasn't my fault! I can't force him to tell me something he doesn't want to tell me. Any more than I can force Rick Sanders."

"You don't have to force him into anything. Just make casual conversation. If you're shy about asking him out, I'll drop a broad hint or two for you."

"Don't you dare!" Thoroughly flustered, Clara wagged a finger in her cousin's face. "Listen to me. I'm not going to throw myself at a man just to get information out of him. That's not fair to him or to me."

"I'm not asking you to *sleep* with him for pity's sake; I just —" Stephanie broke off as a quiet cough sounded from across the store.

Clara swung around to see Frannie standing in the doorway, eyes blinking behind her glasses and her hands dug deep into the pockets of her brown cardigan.

Neither one of them had heard the doorbell. Feeling foolish, Clara smiled at her. How long had the woman been standing there? How much had she heard? She started backtracking the conversation in her mind while Stephanie left the counter and hurried forward.

"Frannie! How are you?"

Frannie sent a worried glance from her to Clara then back to Stephanie again. "Is this a bad time?"

"Oh, goodness, no!" Stephanie laughed and waved a hand at Clara. "Don't take any notice of us. We argue back and forth like that all the time, and we're still the best of friends."

"That's good." Frannie pulled her hands out of her pockets. "I was afraid . . . It's just that we've had enough bad things going on around here. I can't stand hearing people arguing."

"I promise you, no more arguments." Stephanie grinned at Clara. "Right, Cuz?"

"Right." Clara grinned back. "Is there something we can get for you, Frannie?"

As if just remembering why she was there, Frannie nodded.

"I'd like a copy of the Wayne Lester book that just came in."

"Sure. I'll get it for you."

Stephanie darted off, and Frannie shuffled closer to the counter, her thin face looking even more pale as the sunlight fell across her. "It's a nice day outside."

"Very nice." Clara sought for something to say that didn't include a mention of Ana's murder. Before she could come up with something, however, Stephanie had returned with the book.

"I haven't read it yet, of course," she said, as she laid it on the counter, "but I've heard it's every bit as good as his last one."

"I'm looking forward to reading it." Frannie peered at the cover. "He's very good at forecasting the future, you know. He always gives me hope."

Clara scanned the book. "That's something we all need."

"Have you been looking for a new job?" Stephanie asked.

Clara thought for a moment her cousin was going to offer to replace her.

Before she could analyze how she felt about that, Frannie answered, "I'm still working at Jordan's. We're opening up again next Monday. The new owner just moved into town today."

Stephanie pounced on that at once. "New owner? Already? Who is it? Anyone we know?"

"You might. She's been in and out of town a lot lately. Her name is Roberta Prince."

Stephanie wrinkled her brow. "I don't know the name. What's she like?"

"I don't really know her all that well." Frannie's expression suggested she was okay with that. "She's from New York." She said it as if that explained a lot about the woman, and none of it complimentary.

Clara wondered if the comment was somehow directed at her, then decided Frannie was not that subtle. "Have you met her?"

Frannie rolled her eyes. "Oh, yes. She looks like one of those skinny models on magazine covers. You know, fancy blonde hairdo, lots of makeup, expensive clothes. I wouldn't have thought someone like her would ever want to live in Finn's Harbor."

"Oh, I know her!" Stephanie nudged her head at the window. "I've seen her going in and out of Rick's store."

Frannie followed the gesture with a scornful glance. "Yes, she seemed to spend a lot of time over there. Maybe she was trying to buy his business, as well."

Clara raised her eyebrows. "Really?"

Frannie shrugged. "All I know is, she sure wanted Jordan's real bad. She knew Ana was having financial problems, and she was bugging Ana for months to sell the business. I overheard them talking about it in the office. Arguing, I should say. Ana even threatened to sue her for harassment if she didn't leave her alone."

Stephanie exchanged a glance with Clara.

"That *is* weird. I wonder why she wanted Jordan's."

Frannie sniffed. "Whatever it is, it was real important to her. She acted like she'd go to any lengths to get what she wanted. Maybe even . . ." she gulped, then muttered, ". . . murder."

Clara balled her fingers into fists. The voices were back. Whispering, insistent. "Are you saying," she said more loudly than she intended, "that you think Roberta Prince killed Ana to get her business?"

Fear flashed across Frannie's face. "I'm . . . not saying anything. I don't know what happened. I don't want to know." She snatched up her book off the counter and practically ran to the door. "The best thing all of us can do is forget about the whole thing and let the police take care of it." The door closed behind her with a loud snap.

"Well," Stephanie said softly. "What do you make of that?"

Clara cleared her throat. "I think that Frannie's afraid of Roberta Prince and thinks that she killed Ana to get her hands on the business."

"Which is nonsense, of course."

"Of course."

They laughed in unison, though Clara got the impression that she wasn't the only one who wondered if there was a grain of truth in Frannie's ambiguous remarks.

The afternoon seemed to drag for Clara once Stephanie had left. Business was quiet, and she had plenty of time to browse the bookshelves in between customers.

Stephanie's love of all things Poe was obvious. The shelves were stuffed with books by him and about him, and on the wall hung pictures of the author, his house in Philadelphia and his final home in the Bronx.

By the time Clara was ready to close up shop, she had a pretty good idea of where to find everything and was feeling quite pleased with herself as she stepped out into the quiet street and locked the door.

Warmth still rose from the sidewalk, even though the sun had disappeared behind the hills. The breeze from the ocean lifted her hair, cooling her face as she started down toward the parking lot.

She had only taken a few steps when she heard heavy footsteps pounding behind her. Whoever it was, he was catching up fast. Remembering Ana's dead eyes staring up at her, Clara quickened her pace.

The footsteps drew closer.

Voices started whispering in her head. She was tempted to listen, wondering if it was a warning. Surely the killer wouldn't attack her out here on the street, where a car could come along any minute?

The next streetlamp was a few yards away. She probably couldn't outrun him. She'd have to confront him. Wishing she had a gun in her purse, she hurried up to the lamp, then swiftly turned on her pursuer.

Rick Sanders came to a screeching halt just a few yards away, then walked toward her, an odd expression on his face.

Clara let out a shaky breath. The jolt she'd felt when she'd recognized him wasn't entirely fear. Again the voices whispered. Louder this time. *Don't believe anything he says.*

Was that the Quinn Sense, or her own natural instincts kicking in? Before she could make up her mind, he'd reached her.

"Training for the marathon?"

She blinked up at him. He didn't look like a killer. His eyes, gleaming in the light from the streetlamp, held only amusement and something that made her pulse tick a little faster.

"I'm sorry?"

He jerked a thumb over his shoulder. "The way you were hustling back there, I thought you were in training for something."

"Oh, that." She managed a smile. "I was

just in a hurry to get to my car. It's been a long day."

His expression changed to one of concern. "Sorry; did I scare you? It must have shaken all you ladies up quite a bit to find Ana Jordan that way. I don't blame you for scooting down the hill. I should have called out."

At the mention of the dead woman's name, Clara felt a chill. "It wasn't a pleasant experience, by any means." In an attempt to change the subject, she quickly added, "Are you on your way home, too?"

His pause unsettled her. Finally, he said, "As a matter of fact, I was going to stop in at the Pizza Parlor. Care to join me?"

He'd thrown out the invitation casually, as if he'd just thought of it. Clara wasn't fooled for a minute. *Stephanie.*

In spite of everything she'd said, her cousin must have said something to him after all.

"Thank you," she said stiffly. "But my mother will have dinner waiting for me at home." Without waiting for an answer, she turned and sped down the hill.

Safely inside her car, she thumbed Stephanie's number on her cell phone.

Her cousin answered almost right away. "What's wrong?"

"Nothing." Clara waited for her temper to

cool. "At least, not with the store. I thought I told you not to say anything to Rick Sanders about my going out with him."

"I didn't! I swear I didn't!" She paused, then added with growing excitement, "Why? Did he ask you out? Really? What did you say?"

Clara closed her eyes. She didn't need the Quinn Sense to know that Stephanie was telling the truth. She knew her cousin far too well to mistake that tone of voice. "He asked me to go for pizza. I turned him down." She briefly laid her forehead on the steering wheel. He must have thought her a total idiot. "I thought you'd put him up to it."

"Clara! You missed a golden opportunity!"

"No, what I missed was potentially embarrassing myself by asking dumb questions. I'm sorry, Stephanie. I'm not going out with Rick Sanders even if he asks me again, which I seriously doubt after the way I left him tonight."

Stephanie's sigh seemed to hang on the line forever. "I don't see how we're ever going to catch Ana's killer."

"Well, maybe we should just let the police do their job."

"If only you'd use the Quinn Sense —"

"I told you, I can't." Clara softened her

tone. "I'm tired. I'm going home. See you tomorrow." She closed her phone and started the engine. She'd told the truth. She *was* tired, and maybe there was just a little tinge of regret mixed in there as well. It might have been nice to share a pizza with Rick Sanders.

She drove along the coast road, watching the frothy waves turn to silver in the moonlight. No, she'd done the right thing. No more involvements. At least, not for a long time. Long enough for her to forget everything that had happened in New York. Long enough to let go of the past. Until she could do that, she wasn't ready to trust her heart again.

6

Roberta Prince arrived in town the following day. Clara caught sight of her as she strode past the window of the Raven's Nest that afternoon. Stephanie had just left for the day, and Clara was rearranging the window display when the tall blonde passed by.

Frannie was right, Clara thought, as she watched the woman stoop to open the door of Jordan's Stationer's. Roberta Prince did look as if she'd just leapt off the cover of a magazine.

The doorbell rang just then, and she pulled back to greet the customer. To her intense embarrassment, it was Rick Sanders, and he didn't look too happy.

"Is Stephanie here?" he asked, looking around as if he expected to see her pop out from one of the aisles.

"No, she left." Clara did her best to smile as she made her way back to the counter.

"Is there something I can do for you?"

"No . . . Yes . . . No. Thanks." Rick turned back to the door. "I just wanted a word with her, but it can wait."

"I could give her a message." Clara bit her lip. Why was she doing this? Why didn't she just let him go? Because she felt guilty, she answered herself. Should she apologize for cutting him off so rudely last night? Or would that just make her look pathetic?

Rick chose that moment to swing around to face her, catching her off guard. Once more she'd been caught staring at him. Heat rushed to her cheeks, and she started stammering. "I'll be seeing Stephanie later on. I just wondered —"

"Look," Rick began at the same time. "I'm sorry about last night —"

They broke off together, and Clara uttered a sheepish laugh.

"Sorry."

"No, *I'm* sorry." He walked closer to the counter. "I must have scared the heck out of you."

"You didn't." Her violent shake of her head made it spin. "It was just . . ." She trailed off, realizing she couldn't tell him about the misunderstanding.

"It's okay. You don't have to explain." He jerked his head at the wall. "Did I just see

Roberta Prince opening the door of Jordan's?"

"You did." Clara pretended to rearrange a stack of tarot cards. "I heard she just bought the business."

Rick groaned. "I was afraid of that. That woman scares me."

Clara looked up. "She does? Why?"

"I don't know." He headed for the door. "There's just something about her. She's so . . . intense. That much determination can't be good."

Clara smiled. "For her or for you?"

He glanced at her as he opened the door. "For everybody. I'm telling you, that woman's trouble with a capital T."

The door closed behind him, leaving Clara staring at the space where he'd been. He'd sounded genuinely disturbed by the new owner of Jordan's Stationer's. She wondered what had gone on between those two to upset him so much. Had she been pressuring him, too, about selling his business?

When she called Stephanie later to tell her about the encounter, her cousin seized on Rick's words. "Whoa — a tough woman. Maybe Frannie wasn't so far off base, after all. I wonder if she was in town last Friday?"

"If you're expecting me to ask her, you're

out of luck."

Once more she was treated to Stephanie's exaggerated sigh.

"We're getting nowhere fast. We need to sit down together and work out what we're going to do. I know it's your day off tomorrow, but come over to the store in the morning for coffee. Molly will be there, and hopefully we won't be busy and we can all get together."

"All right. I'll see you then." Clara closed up her phone, wondering what her cousin hoped to accomplish. They might as well face it. They were amateurs, messing in business best left for the police. Frannie was right. They should just forget about it and let Dan handle it.

Hoping to take her mind off things, she spent the evening with her mother watching a TV crime movie. Not that it helped much, since Jessie insisted on making sarcastic comments about the stupidity of the investigators.

Arriving at the Raven's Nest the next morning, Clara was all set to persuade Stephanie to give up on the investigation. She was barely inside the door, however, when Stephanie rushed over to her.

"Thank goodness you're here. There are no customers right now. We've really got to get moving on this." She took Clara's arm and steered her down the aisle to the Reading Nook.

Molly sat slumped in an armchair, her face drawn in misery.

Clara sat down next to her, while Stephanie hurried over to the coffee urn to fill up the mugs.

"Molly's been kicked out of her reading group," she said, handing a steaming mug to Clara.

Clara turned to Molly, who gave her a miserable nod. "Why on earth would they do that?"

"They think I killed Ana, of course." Molly pushed her bangs back with an unsteady hand. "Pretty soon everybody in town is going to boycott me."

"Did they actually say that was the reason?" Clara asked her.

"Not in so many words." Molly took the mug from Stephanie's hand. "What they said was that they no longer felt I fitted in with the group, and it would be better for everyone if I didn't come again."

Clara groaned. "This is ridiculous."

Tears glistened in Molly's eyes as she put down her coffee.

"I can't even walk down the street without people staring at me and whispering to each other. I don't know how much more of this I can take." She got up from her chair and fled around the corner.

"Do you think she's gone back there to cry?" Stephanie worried at her bottom lip as she gazed after her friend. "I feel so bad for her. What are we going to do?"

Clara sipped her coffee before putting it down. She'd heard the note of reproach in her cousin's voice and knew it was directed at her. "We're doing everything we can," she said quietly.

"No, we're not." Stephanie turned to her, blue eyes accusing. "Not everything."

Clara drew a deep breath. Somewhere in the back of her mind she'd known it would come to this. To help Molly, she would have to sacrifice her own peace of mind — everything she had fought against for years — with no guarantee that she could solve Molly's problem.

"All right. I get it." She shook her head. "I don't like it, but I get it. I can't make any promises, but I guess I can try. It's just that it's been such a long time, and I don't know how well it will work anymore."

Stephanie sat up, excitement now gleaming in her eyes. "You'll do it? You'll use the Quinn Sense?"

Just hearing the words spoken made Clara

shiver. "I'll try. That's all I can tell you. But I should warn you, you might not like what you hear."

Stephanie frowned. "What does that mean?"

Clara hesitated, then said slowly, "Molly. I heard the voices, just briefly, when she said she'd gone straight home from here on Friday night. I don't know what they were trying to tell me because I shut them out, but I do know that Molly wasn't telling the truth."

Stephanie was about to answer when Molly returned, her eyes red and weepy. "Sorry," she muttered. "I don't usually let things get to me like that."

Stephanie reached for a box of tissues on the counter next to her and handed it to Molly. "It's all right. Sit down and take a deep breath; then answer a question for us."

Molly frowned. "What's the question?"

"Are you quite sure you didn't see anything unusual on Friday night?"

For a moment it seemed that Molly wasn't going to answer; then she let out her breath in a rush. "I already told you I didn't. Why? What have you heard?"

"Nothing." Stephanie exchanged an uneasy glance with Clara.

"It's just that, well, you seemed a little

unsure of yourself when Dan questioned you and —"

"Oh, all right!" Molly blew her nose and tucked the tissue in her pocket. "Maybe I didn't go straight home that night."

Stephanie's eyebrows shot up. "You lied to Dan?"

"I had to." Molly sniffed and stared at the floor. "I was meeting Jason."

Clara looked at her cousin for help.

Stephanie looked as if she were about to explode. "Molly Owens! I thought that was over long ago."

Molly shrugged. "We got back together."

Clara leaned forward. "Who's Jason?"

"A very bad influence on a young woman," Stephanie said, in her prim mom's voice. "He's a biker, and he's trying to turn Molly into a biker babe."

"There's nothing wrong with that!" Molly protested.

"There is when you're riding with some-one who drinks too much, probably takes drugs and likes to beat up people."

"I take it you've met this Jason," Clara said.

Stephanie rolled her eyes. "Yes, and I don't like him."

"I'm twenty-one," Molly pointed out. "Old enough to take care of myself. It's nobody's business but mine who I go out with, and I wasn't breaking any laws."

"Then why did you lie to Dan about going home?"

Molly paused, then muttered, "I didn't want to get Jason into trouble."

"There, you see?" Stephanie flung out a hand in a dramatic gesture. "Now who says you had nothing to hide?"

"It's just that Dan has it in for Jason, and he'll use any excuse to come down hard on him. I just thought I would save everybody a lot of hassle if I kept quiet about seeing him that night."

Clara waited, torn between hoping to hear the voices and fearing that she would. When her mind remained silent, she asked, "Where did you see Jason?"

"We met down at the harbor." Molly flashed her a defiant look. "If you're thinking that Jason might have had something to do with Ana's death, you're dead wrong. He didn't go anywhere near here. He lives in West Ridge, in the opposite direction. I saw him leave. Besides, he didn't even know Ana."

"All right, I —" Clara broke off as the doorbell jingled. "A customer." She got to her feet. "I'll go."

Stephanie flapped a hand at her. "Let

whoever it is look around first. The longer they browse, the more likely they are to buy."

Clara sank back on her chair. "Good thinking."

"That's why I'm successful." Stephanie turned to Molly. "Look, I'm sorry, Molly, but you shouldn't have lied to the police. I think you should —"

"Hell-o-o-o!"

The woman's voice had floated down from the front of the store. Clara pushed herself up from the chair. "Stay there. I'll see what she wants."

Hurrying up the aisle, Clara caught a glimpse of the customer. Short blonde hair, pale beige suit, bright orange shirt under the jacket. She didn't need to see the woman's face to know that they were being honored with the presence of the new owner of Jordan's Stationer's.

"Good morning!" Clara stepped up behind the counter and gave the woman a bright smile. "What can I do for you?"

A pair of sharp blue eyes dissected her from head to waist.

"Who are you?"

Clara raised her chin. "I'm Clara Quinn. Who are you?"

"I'm the new owner of the store next door.

Roberta Prince." She sent a disparaging glance around the shelves, lingering on the raven for a moment or two before turning back to Clara. "Are you the owner of this store?"

"No, she isn't. I am."

Stephanie had crept up on them unheard, and Roberta Prince swung around to look at her. "What time do you close?"

Stephanie looked confused. "Excuse me?"

"I said, what time do you close?" Roberta waved a perfectly manicured hand at the door, rattling the gold charm bracelet on her wrist. "I don't want to close before you do, but on the other hand, I don't want to hang around there all night, either."

"We close at eight," Clara answered for her cousin. "Six on Saturdays and Sundays."

The piercing gaze swung back to her. "Fair enough. What about the hardware store across the street?"

Stephanie moved closer. "What about it?"

The look she got from Roberta would have shrunk an armadillo. "What . . . time . . . does . . . he . . . close?"

Clara held her breath as Stephanie's cheeks flushed at the patronizing tone. "Same as us, of course."

"Fine." Roberta narrowed her eyes as she gazed at the table holding the cookbooks. "I thought you sold that weird paranormal stuff."

"We do. We also sell craft books and cookbooks." Stephanie paused, then added, "Though I'm sure none of that could possibly have any interest for you."

As if recognizing an adversary when she saw one, Roberta's bright-red mouth twisted in a humorless smile. "Actually, I'm an excellent cook. Just ask the hunk who owns the hardware store across the street."

Stephanie still hadn't closed her mouth when the door closed behind Roberta with a soft thud.

Clara was trying to analyze the ache in her midriff when her cousin exploded. "Of all the nerve! Who does she think she is waltzing in here with her designer suit and expensive perfume and insulting us like that?"

"Take no notice of her."

"How can I ignore that?" Stephanie stared at the door as if she expected the offending woman to walk back in at any minute. "What was all that about asking Rick if she's a good cook, anyway?"

Again the ache. Clara rubbed her stomach. "I imagine she was trying to let us know that she's cooked dinner for him or something."

"What?" Stephanie almost choked on the word. "I don't believe it. Rick would never go for that puffed-up phony. She's got to be lying."

Remembering her last conversation with Rick, Clara was inclined to agree. On the other hand, Rick could have said all that stuff about Roberta to hide the fact that they were close. "Not that it matters to us, of course," she said, knowing deep down that it mattered to her. "It's none of our business who she invites to dinner."

"It is our business when they're both murder suspects."

"Who's a suspect?" Molly joined them at the counter. "Who was that just now?"

"That was the new owner of Jordan's Stationer's." Stephanie quickly filled Molly in on everything Frannie had said about Roberta Prince. "It also seems she's on intimate terms with Rick Sanders," she said, while Clara pretended not to hear that.

"They could be conspirators," Molly said, looking hopeful. "Maybe they were working together to get rid of Ana."

Clara sighed. "All this speculation is getting us nowhere. We need to do something constructive if we're ever going to find our killer."

"I thought we were doing something

constructive," Stephanie said, giving her a meaningful look.

"Besides that." Clara hoped her frown would warn her cousin not to say anything about the Quinn Sense. "For instance, if Molly didn't let Ana into the store, then someone else must have. Someone who must have had a key, since there was no sign of a break-in."

Molly's face brightened. "I would think the new owner would have the keys."

"She wasn't the new owner until after Ana died," Stephanie said.

"We don't know that." Clara leaned her elbows on the counter. "What if Ana had already signed over the store to her? She could have given Roberta the keys then."

Stephanie dismissed that with a wave of her hand. "Then why would Roberta Prince need to kill her?"

"Maybe she killed her for some other reason. Think about it. Roberta took over the store awfully fast after Ana died. I wouldn't think a business could change hands that quickly, with all the red tape and paperwork involved."

Molly nodded. "She's right. It would have taken longer than a couple of days."

"So let's assume that Roberta had the keys." Clara tapped the counter with her fingers while she concentrated. "Also assuming she had a motive, why would she kill Ana in here? Why not in her own store and make it look like a robbery or something?"

"Maybe she wanted to put the blame on someone else." Stephanie glanced at Molly. "She could have heard about the fight you had with Ana that morning. After all, enough people heard you threaten her. Maybe she lured Ana into the stockroom and hit her over the head with your bust hoping you'd get the blame for it."

"It's possible," Clara said, grasping at any straw that would eliminate Rick Sanders as a suspect.

Stephanie gave her a hard stare. "Anything?"

Knowing that her cousin was asking about the voices, Clara shook her head. Molly's curious glance unsettled her, and she said quickly, "Okay, so who else might have a key to the store?"

"John Halloran," Molly said, moving closer to them. "He used to shut up shop for Ana when she was out of town. He must have had a key at some point. He could have kept it all this time."

Clara grabbed that straw, too. "Right! He could have heard Molly threaten Ana and decided to make use of the key."

"Also possible," Stephanie murmured. "But what about Rick Sanders? He used to work for Ana's father. He could have kept a key as well. He could have easily overheard Molly's screaming match on Friday morning. He was outside his store, remember?"

Clara's shoulders sagged. "Right. I remember."

"So," Stephanie said brightly, "we are right back where we started. Three suspects, all with possible motives. This is getting really complicated."

"Well, they could all have had the means," Molly put in. "The key to the store."

"Again," Clara said, "we don't know that for sure."

"Which leaves us with opportunity." Stephanie fixed Clara with another hard stare. "We have to find out if any of our suspects have alibis."

The doorbell jingled, making them all jump.

Mrs. Riley poked a disapproving face around the door. "I heard you got Wayne Lester's new book in," she said, glaring at Molly.

"Yes, we do. I'll get it for you." Stephanie twisted around and disappeared down the aisle.

"Keep that woman away from me," Mrs. Riley said, still hovering in the doorway. "I don't want her anywhere near me."

"Don't worry," Molly muttered, turning her back on the elderly woman. "I don't want to be around you, either."

Clara was about to answer when Stephanie reappeared with the book in her hand. She laid it on the counter, saying to Mrs. Riley, "I've heard it's just as good as his last one."

The words seemed to ring a bell in Clara's head. Even as she reached for the book, her hand began to tingle. The voices were soft, quiet, whispering in muffled tones that made no sense.

Out of habit, she began to shut them out, but then she remembered her promise. Closing her eyes, she relaxed her mind, concentrating on the elusive words. Something to do with the book and the words Stephanie had spoken. *I've heard it's just as good as his last one.*

Stephanie had said pretty much the same words to Frannie. Two days ago. The voices whispered louder. Clara frowned, trying to hear them. What were they trying to tell her?

"Well, are you going to stand there all day or are you going to take my money?"

Mrs. Riley's voice scattered her thoughts.

Clara blinked, and the voices faded away. Behind the irritated customer, Stephanie was staring, her face full of expectation.

"I'm sorry." Clara snatched up the book and slid it across the scanner. "That'll be twenty-one ninety-five."

Mrs. Riley uttered a sound of disgust. "Ridiculous price for a book. I could buy three paperbacks for that price." She snatched the bag from Clara and, still muttering to herself, marched out of the shop.

Stephanie barely waited for the door to close behind her before bounding over to the counter. "You heard something, didn't you? The Quinn Sense. I saw it in your face."

Clara sent a wary look at the aisles, but Molly had disappeared. Hopefully, she was finishing her coffee in the Reading Nook. "Shhh!" Clara scowled at her cousin. "You swore you'd keep quiet about that, remember?"

"Sorry." Stephanie glanced over her shoulder. "I got excited." She leaned forward and added in a whisper, "You did hear something, though, right?"

Clara gave her a brief nod. "Not much, though. It was more a feeling than actually hearing anything. It had something to do with what you said to Mrs. Riley."

Stephanie looked bewildered. "Mrs. Riley? Surely you don't think she could have killed Ana? She's just a frail old lady."

"It wouldn't take much strength to lift that bust and bring it down hard enough to kill."

Stephanie puffed out her breath. "Now you're being ridiculous. We're beginning to suspect everybody who comes into this store. You'll be saying next that I could have killed Ana."

Clara tilted her head on one side. "You do have an alibi, don't you?"

"Of course I do! What —" She broke off with a laugh. "Okay, enough of the dark humor. This is serious business. We have to find out where everybody was that night and what they were doing." Her expression grew serious. "You have to go out with Rick Sanders now. It's the only way we can find out where he was."

Clara rolled her eyes. "I'm leaving. I have an apartment to look at."

She headed for the door, and Stephanie followed her. "I thought you decided to stay at home with your mom."

"I changed my mind." Clara paused at the door. "When I got home last night, I found some of my stuff in my room had been moved around. My dear mother said she was tidying up the house, but I know she was snooping. I've got to find somewhere where I can have some privacy."

Stephanie made a face. "I'm sorry, Clara. I'm sure she's just concerned about you."

"Yeah, well, I'm not sixteen years old anymore. She can ask me what she needs to know instead of poking around my personal stuff."

Waving good-bye, Clara stepped out into the street. The familiar smell of damp sand and seaweed greeted her, and she stood for a moment, enjoying the soft touch of the sea breeze on her face.

She'd lost count of the times she'd stood on a busy corner in Manhattan amid the rank odor of diesel fuel, burning tires and exhaust fumes, longing to be back in Finn's Harbor breathing clean, cool sea air.

Now she was home, with a whole day to enjoy the waning summer, and she intended to do just that. Forget the morbid events of the past few days, ignore the Quinns' bizarre family gift, if it could be called that, and just be a normal, contented person with a few hours to kill in one of the most picturesque towns in New England. With that, she set off down the hill to her car.

7

Clara drove along the coast road until she'd left the town of Finn's Harbor behind. Ahead of her, still out of sight, lay Sealwich Bay, a small fishing port known for its abundance of lobsters.

She hadn't had a lobster roll since the last time she'd visited from New York, and just the thought of them made her mouth water. The best lobster rolls in the world were made at Hannegan's, a small restaurant overlooking the ocean, and she couldn't wait to taste one again.

As the scenery unfolded in a never-ending display of mountains, craggy shoreline and tiny islands dotting the ocean, she reminded herself again how lucky she was to be living in such magnificent and peaceful surroundings.

True, there were occasions when she missed the stores, the theaters and the crowded restaurants of the big city, the excitement of never knowing what was around the corner, the ever-changing scenarios of people from all walks of life and from all over the world filling the crowded sidewalks.

Not enough to go back, however. Right now she was supremely happy to be sailing along the coast road, with nothing but sea and sky to distract her mind.

Pulling into Hannegan's tiny parking lot, she was pleased to see only two cars and a pickup parked there. That meant she'd have a good chance of a window table.

The spicy aroma from the busy kitchen tantalized her appetite as she pushed open the door and walked inside. A cheerful young woman dressed in a pink uniform showed her to the last vacant table by the window, and Clara settled down to enjoy her lunch.

From where she sat, she could just catch a glimpse of the light twinkling from Cape Neddick's Light. She watched it, mesmerized by the insistent flash every six seconds, and didn't notice the tall figure approach her table until he spoke.

"This is a pleasant surprise!"

She looked up, straight into the eyes of Rick Sanders.

For a wild moment she thought Stephanie

must have sent him, then remembered her cousin had no idea that she had driven to Sealwich. Realizing she'd gone far too long without answering him, she blurted out, "What are you doing here?"

Apart from a slightly raised eyebrow, Rick seemed unaffected by the abrupt question. "I'm picking up supplies for the store. The warehouse where I get my garden tools only delivers once a week, and I had a run on pitchforks and rakes. Guess people are getting ready for the fall."

It was none of her business, of course, and all she could do was keep nodding throughout his long explanation. When he paused, she felt obligated to return the favor.

"I came up here for a lobster roll. They make the best ones on the coast here."

"Ah, well then, I'll have to give it a shot." He gestured to the vacant chair opposite her. "Mind if I join you?"

Yes, she did mind. She wanted to be alone, to think things through and decide how she was going to handle her cousin's daunting expectations of her.

It would be rude to turn him away, though, especially after their previous encounter. Already he was getting the uncomfortable look on his face that people got when they suspected they'd made an embarrassing mistake. "Sure." She waved a hand at the chair.

He still looked uncertain as he sat down, and she began to feel ashamed of her behavior. Bad enough that she'd practically run away from him in the street. But now she was acting as if he were intruding on her privacy.

In an effort to make amends, she smiled at him. "I hear the hardware store is doing well."

"It is." His face relaxed a little. "Then again, I'm the only hardware store in town, so I guess I have a bit of a monopoly."

"So who's looking after it now?"

"Oh, I have someone who comes in now and again when I need to take off. John's an old fogy, but he gets the job done."

"John?"

She'd asked the question idly, more to keep the conversation going than anything. She was taking a sip of water when he answered.

"John Halloran. He used to own a candy store on Main Street, where the Pizza Parlor is now, so he knows how to handle a store."

Clara choked on the water, and had to gasp for air, while Rick watched her with an odd expression on his face.

"You okay?" he asked at last, and she nodded.

Her voice sounded hoarse when she answered. "I remember the candy store."

"Oh, you know John, then."

"Yes." She hesitated, then added quickly, "Not very well, though."

Rick's gaze seemed to be probing her mind. "Anything I should know?"

She could feel her cheeks growing warm. She couldn't tell him she suspected John Halloran of murdering Ana Jordan. After all, Rick was a suspect as well. She could hear Stephanie's voice in her head. *Get what you can out of him.*

She had to say something. Anything. He was looking at her again with that weird look on his face. She opened her mouth to speak, but just then the waitress brought her lobster roll.

To Clara's relief, Rick transferred his attention to the waitress while he ordered his roll and a beer. She tried to think clearly, striving for a way to find out what he was doing on Friday night.

"Can I get you something else?"

At the sound of his voice, she looked up with a start to find him watching her again. "Oh, thank you, no." She glanced at the waitress, who was unashamedly sizing up her new customer.

"That'll be it, then," Rick said, giving the young woman a smile that sent her dancing off for his order.

"Sure you're okay?"

Clara avoided his gaze. "I'm fine." It had come out a little too abrupt and she hurried to add, "Just a little preoccupied, I guess."

"I can imagine. The shock of finding Ana's body and all. It takes a long time to get something like that out of your head."

"Exactly." She felt herself beginning to relax. "That's why I came out here. To get away from it all for a little while."

"Has Dan made any progress on finding the killer?"

Her nerves tightened again. "I wouldn't know. He doesn't confide in us."

"I just wondered if you'd heard rumors."

"Such as?"

He shrugged. "Oh, I don't know. People talk."

She didn't like where this conversation was going. He seemed much too interested in knowing if there'd been any developments in the case. Or maybe she was just overreacting again. She seemed to be doing that a lot lately.

She took a big bite of her lobster roll, spilling some of the lobster pieces onto her plate. "That's the problem with these things," she mumbled. "You can't look elegant while you're eating them."

"You could look elegant hauling lobsters out of the ocean."

He was smiling. He really did have a nice smile. She couldn't help smiling back. "Thank you. I think."

The waitress arrived with Rick's order, giving Clara time to recover her composure. She waited until he had started on his roll before saying as casually as she could manage, "What really surprises me about Ana's murder is that apparently no one saw anything, or noticed anything unusual. Dan said she was killed sometime between nine and eleven on Friday night. There must have been people on the street around that time."

Rick lifted his glass. "What do you mean by unusual?"

"Well, you know, Ana going into the bookstore after hours. Maybe forced to go in by someone."

"How do you know she went in after hours?" He tilted the glass and drank several gulps of his beer.

Clara paused, her roll halfway to her mouth. "Are you saying you believe the rumors that Molly killed her?"

She couldn't read his expression as he looked at her. "It's obvious you don't."

"Of course I don't." She put down her roll, her appetite for it fast disappearing. "I think the whole idea is ridiculous. Molly had nothing to do with Ana's murder."

"She told you that."

"Yes, she did."

"And you believed her."

"Absolutely. I can usually tell when people are lying."

"Then you're lucky. Personally, I think there are far too many good liars in this world."

The bitterness in his words was impossible to ignore. Someone somewhere must have hurt him badly. She knew how that felt. She could literally feel the resentment steaming out of him. It was such a contrast to his usual disposition that it shocked her into silence.

"Sorry." He grinned, and in a flash once more became the cheerful, agreeable man she thought she knew. "As a matter of fact, I agree with you. I just can't see Molly bashing someone over the head with a masterpiece she'd just created."

Clara's shoulders sagged in relief. With or without the Sense, she was ready to believe that Rick Sanders was not the killer either, and until the voices told her otherwise, she intended to hold on to that. "So who do you think might have been responsible?"

"Could have been anyone, I guess."

He turned to look out of the window, giving her an opportunity to study his profile. Strong nose and chin. She liked that.

"So, have you met the formidable Roberta Prince?"

His question took her by surprise, especially since he looked back at her and once more caught her staring at him. He had to think she was totally juvenile. "Yes, she came into the store this morning and introduced herself. Sort of."

Rick smiled. "Gave you a hard time?"

She hesitated, remembering the flamboyant woman's words. *Just ask the hunk who owns the hardware store across the street.*

"Not really. As you said, though, she's a bit . . . intimidating."

"I know what you mean."

He'd sounded grim, and Clara frowned, wondering who to believe. Roberta had made it sound like they were on hugging terms. *Come on, Sense, where are you when I need you?* "She mentioned you, actually."

She'd unsettled him. His eyebrows twitched, and his fingers did a little dance on his glass. "Really. What did she have to say about me, exactly?"

"Not a lot. Just that she'd cooked dinner for you." She was feeling uncomfortable herself now. He must know she was fishing for information. Then again, that's what she was supposed to do. It had nothing to do with her own personal interest. It made her feel better to think that, anyway.

"Yes, she did." He uttered a soft sound that could have been disgust. "She manipulated me into it, if you want the truth. She arrived on my doorstep with bags of food and proceeded to take over my kitchen. I couldn't throw her out without looking like a jerk, so I let her stay." He looked out the window again, his lower lip jutting out.

He was holding something back. Something he didn't want her to know. Had Roberta stayed the night?

She shut down the Sense before it could tell her anything else. There were some things she'd rather not know. She kept the conversation on safer ground after that, and it was a relief when Rick finally drained his beer and glanced at his watch.

"I've gotta go. They'll be waiting for me at the warehouse."

"Me, too. I'm supposed to be apartment hunting." She reached for the bill, but he grabbed it first.

131

"My treat."

"Oh, no, I couldn't . . ."

"Of course you can. You can return the favor sometime." He got to his feet, waiting for her to step out into the narrow space between the tables. "Maybe the Pizza Parlor for dinner some night?"

She nodded, anxious to escape the curious gazes of the young couple at the next table. Hurrying out into the bright sunshine, she headed for her car. Rick called out to her as she climbed inside, and she waved at him before turning on the engine. He was right behind her in a red pickup as she drove out of the parking lot and onto the road. He followed her for a couple of blocks before turning off onto one of the side streets, apparently on his way to the warehouse.

She thought about their conversation on the way back to town. Mostly about the few words they'd had about Roberta Prince. Apparently Rick and Roberta didn't share the same vision of their relationship. Unless one of them was lying. Not that it mattered, of course. None of it had any bearing on Ana's murder.

It occurred to her then that she still had no idea where Rick was on Friday night. *Was he with Roberta?* "Stop that!" she said out loud, angry with herself for the self-torture.

It wasn't that she had any feelings for him, she assured herself. It was just that if the two of them were together that night, they would both have an alibi. *Or maybe not.* Again she shut down the voice. She just couldn't accept the idea that Rick might have helped Roberta murder Ana Jordan.

She rounded a bend and came face-to-face with her favorite view — a huge sweep of the bay, with red roofs and white walls sparkling in the sun, and green mountains rising up behind them. The sight never failed to raise her spirits, and she was smiling as she drove into the little town of Finn's Harbor.

Stephanie wandered into the living room and threw herself down on the couch, bouncing George hard enough to rattle his newspaper.

He lowered it and stared at her over the rims of his reading glasses. "What's up now?"

"Nothing." She sighed and leaned back against the couch's firm cushions. "Everything. The kids hate school, the back-to-school sale fizzled out and we're no closer to finding out who killed Ana and clearing

Molly's name."

George wrinkled his brow. "Ethan and Olivia always hate school the first week or so after summer break. They'll settle down. What about Michael? I thought he'd love kindergarten."

"Well, he doesn't." Stephanie reached for her soda and took a long drink from the glass. "He misses Olivia. You know he's followed her around everywhere ever since he could walk."

George shook his newspaper and retreated behind it again. "It will do him good to go it alone. Make him more independent."

Stephanie glared at him through the back page. "George Henry Dowd, put that newspaper down. I need to talk, and we never seem to get more than five minutes together lately."

George sighed and slowly folded up the newspaper. "All right. I'm all ears."

Stephanie resisted the temptation to tease him. George was sensitive about his prominent ears. "I'm worried about the bookstore. We had only four customers today, and only two of them bought anything."

"You've had slow days before."

"I know." She studied her feet, wondering if her slippers would hold up until Christmas, when she would get a new pair from her mother, as usual. "But this time it feels different. I think people are avoiding the store because of Ana's murder."

"I think you're worrying about nothing, as usual." He slipped an arm across her shoulders. "Everything will turn out all right; you'll see."

"It won't if the customers stay away."

"You just had a slow day, that's all. You've had plenty of them before, and then people always make up for it and you're rushed off your feet."

"I hope you're right."

"Of course I'm right. Aren't I always?"

She smiled up at him. "Of course you are, George."

"So will you stop worrying now?"

Her smile faded. "I'll stop worrying when Ana Jordan's killer is behind bars."

"I guess Dan hasn't gotten any further with the investigation, or we would have heard something."

"He still thinks Molly killed her."

George hesitated and she braced for his next words. "Honey, you know there's always a chance that Molly —"

"No!" She turned on him, unable to stem her frustration. "Why is everyone so quick to condemn Molly? What has that girl ever done to deserve all this accusation?"

"She threatened Ana the morning she died," George said quietly. "It wasn't the first time she'd yelled threats at her, either."

"Just words, that's all. You know Molly. She's got a quick temper, and she's vocal when she's mad, but you know she's not a killer."

"Who knows what anyone is capable of, given enough provocation?"

"Well, Ana Jordan was good at provoking people. I'll say that for her." Stephanie slumped back against the cushions again. "There are plenty of people out there who could have hated her enough to kill her. Even you."

George's voice rose a notch. "Me? What does that mean?"

"You went out with her in high school before you started dating me, didn't you?"

"Well, yes, but I —"

"And you dumped her. And why was that again?"

"I've told you more than once. She got too possessive. She wanted to know what I was doing every minute I was away from her. When she started questioning my friends about where I was and what I was doing, I decided she wasn't worth the hassle."

"And she made your life miserable for

136

weeks after that, right?"

"Well, yeah, but it was worth it to be rid of her." He pulled her closer. "Besides, by then I'd spotted this hot little cheerleader and was getting to know her better."

Stephanie grinned. "I remember that skinny basketball player leering at me from across the court."

"Leering?"

"Leering. Like this." She gave him her best imitation of a teenage ogle.

He shook his head. "If I looked at you like that, I'm surprised you ever agreed to go out with me."

"You were the star basketball player. How could I resist?" She leaned her head against his shoulder. After a moment she murmured, "I just wish all this Ana business was over with, and we could get back to normal."

"Dan's a good cop. He'll get at the truth eventually."

"I hope you're right." She was almost tempted to tell him that she and Clara were on the trail of the killer with Molly's help, but she knew what his reaction would be — nothing short of an erupting volcano. George Dowd was as sweet a man as she'd ever met, but his red hair matched up to the myth. Upset him enough and his temper was spectacular.

Best to keep quiet about it and just hope that he never found out what they were up to, or the sparks would fly for sure.

8

After spending the evening helping her mother clean house, Clara was looking forward the next morning to retreating to the peace and quiet of the Raven's Nest. Jessie had been even more difficult than usual, giving Clara all kinds of advice about finding a man and settling down before she got too old to raise a family.

"You're wasting your life burying yourself among all those musty old books," she'd declared, ignoring Clara's pleas to change the subject. "I don't know why you left New York. There are so many more opportunities there."

Clara knew that was her mother's way of saying there were more eligible men in the city. More men perhaps, but the right man had been just as elusive there as in Finn's Harbor. In fact, she was beginning to doubt there was a right man anywhere out there for her. A man she could respect and trust with her heart. That kind of man was tough to find.

Stephanie greeted her at the door with the news that Molly was sick and hadn't come in that morning. "I have to leave pretty soon to pick up Michael from kindergarten," she added, following Clara behind the counter. "It's been pretty quiet, so you should be okay on your own. If you get really swamped, call me, and I'll try to get back here."

"I'll be fine," Clara assured her. More than fine, she thought, as Stephanie grabbed her purse and flew out the door. She would have the whole place to herself for the rest of the day. At least, in between customers.

After straightening the shelves, which took no time at all since they had been barely touched, she wandered to the Reading Nook and brewed a fresh pot of coffee. She had no sooner sat down with the local newspaper when the doorbell's chimes announced a customer.

Sighing, Clara dropped the *Harbor Chronicle* on the coffee table and hurried to the front of the store. Frannie stood at the counter and seemed surprised to see her.

"Oh, I thought Stephanie would be here," she said, looking past Clara's shoulder as if expecting Stephanie to appear.

"She had to leave." Clara walked behind the counter and gave the nervous little woman a smile. "Can I help you with something?"

"Yes, I . . . ah . . . Maybe I should wait until Stephanie comes back." Frannie glanced back at the window and turned to leave.

"She's gone for the day, I'm afraid."

Frannie answered her, but her words seemed to come from a long way off.

Clara clenched the desk in front of her as the dreaded familiar sensations crept over her. She could hear the voices, whispering, trying to tell her something. Habit prompted her to close her mind to them, but they were insistent.

Frannie knew something. Something important.

"Ah . . . Would you like a cup of coffee? It's fresh. I just made it."

Frannie paused, obviously trying to make up her mind.

Clara tried again. "I could use some company. It gets lonely on my own. Things have been really quiet in here lately."

With noticeable reluctance, Frannie turned to look at her. "Well, all right, but only for a few minutes. Roberta doesn't like me taking long breaks."

"Oh, of course." Clara led the way down the aisle. "I thought Jordan's wasn't opening again until Monday."

"That's our opening day, but there's a lot to do before then." Frannie took the corner seat and huddled down on it as if she were cold. "Roberta is changing a lot of things."

More out of curiosity than anything, Clara asked, "Has the sale actually gone through, then? It seems awfully fast. Roberta must have a very good lawyer."

Frannie took the mug Clara handed her and swallowed a mouthful of coffee, apparently without noticing it was steaming hot.

Clara winced when she saw Frannie's eyes watering. That must have stung.

"Yes, well, that's what I came to tell Stephanie." Frannie looked over her shoulder, her eyes switching from side to side as she skimmed the aisle. "I guess it'll be okay to tell you, only please, don't tell a soul you heard it from me."

Intrigued now, Clara held a hand to her chest. "Of course. I swear."

Frannie put the mug down on the table. "I did some filing for Roberta this morning."

Wondering where this was leading, Clara nodded. "That's nice."

"She had a lot of official papers among

the bills and correspondence. I was sorting through them when she came into the office and snatched them out of my hand."

Clara raised her eyebrows. "Snatched them?"

Frannie nodded, and for a moment Clara thought she might start crying, but then she raised her chin. "She said she'd left them on the desk by mistake and that she'd take care of them herself."

Clara was beginning to see a glimmer of light. "Ah. They were papers she didn't want you to see."

"Yes." Frannie leaned back as if she'd just got a load off her shoulders.

Clara hesitated, then ventured a guess. "You think there was something suspicious about that?"

"I don't think. I know."

Excitement rippled through Clara's veins. This was what the Sense had been trying to tell her. Frannie did know something. "You read the papers."

"One of them, yes." Once more Frannie glanced up and down the aisle. "It was a contract, and Ana had signed it. It said that Roberta lent her a lot of money to settle her debts, on condition that if Ana couldn't turn the store around in six months, or if something happened to her that she couldn't manage the store, then Jordan's Stationer's would automatically belong to Roberta."

Clara held her breath so long her ears started to buzz. There it was. The motive. "Jordan's was showing a profit before Ana died?" It was more a statement than a question.

Frannie picked up her coffee and took a cautious sip. "Yes," she said, as she lowered the mug. "Ana was excited that things seemed to be turning around. She was even talking about celebrating with a trip to Portland." She stared earnestly at Clara. "Do you think I should tell Dan? He was in the store yesterday, asking a lot of questions. He said if I thought of anything else to call him."

Clara shifted on her chair. "I think you should do whatever feels right," she said at last.

Frannie seemed disappointed with her answer. "It just seems weird that just when things were doing better and it looked like Ana would keep Jordan's after all, something really bad happens to her, and Roberta ends up with the store."

Secretly Clara agreed with her, but without more proof, she drew the line at actually accusing the woman of murder. "Well, I guess it wouldn't hurt to mention it to Dan.

Though I think it will take a lot more than that for him to actually do anything about it."

"What I'm afraid of is that he'd tell Roberta that I told him. She'd waste no time in firing me, I'm sure. Or worse." Frannie glanced at her watch and got up. "I thought perhaps Stephanie could tell him, without mentioning she heard it from me."

Pushing herself up from her chair, Clara said as evenly as she could manage, "I don't think Stephanie would want to do that. If you feel threatened, then the best thing to do is not say anything to anyone. If Roberta did kill Ana, Dan will eventually find out and come asking questions. Then you can tell him what you saw."

Frannie obviously wasn't happy when she muttered, "Okay, but I tell you, that woman will do just about anything to get what she wants. Anyone who takes classes in auto repair just to meet men is not my idea of a good person. Thanks for the coffee."

Clara barely waited for the door to close behind her before calling Stephanie. "What do you think?" she said, after she'd finished repeating the entire conversation with Frannie. "Do you think Frannie should tell Dan about the contract?"

Stephanie's sigh echoed down the line.

"Well, it does give Roberta a motive to get rid of Ana. But enough to kill her? I don't know what Dan could do without proof. He must have questioned Roberta, and we don't even know if she was in town that night."

Rick would know. For a moment the voice was so clear Clara thought she had said the words out loud. She closed her eyes, refusing to listen, and jumped when Stephanie's voice rang in her ear.

"Clara, are you okay?"

"I'm fine." She shook her head to clear it.

"I thought I heard you groaning."

"I bumped my elbow on the counter."

Stephanie accepted the lie, much to Clara's relief. "Ouch. I know how that hurts. So, what are we going to do about Roberta?"

The doorbell jangled, startling her again. It didn't help to see John Halloran walking toward her. "I have to go," she said quickly. "I have a customer." She hung up before Stephanie could answer.

John raised his hand at her and disappeared down one of the aisles.

Clara waited for him to return, trying to look busy by going through a pile of books that had been reserved by customers and not yet picked up.

The one on the top was Wayne Lester's astrology book. Clara picked it up, and immediately the voices started whispering again.

She stared at the cover, trying hard to hear what it was the Sense was trying to tell her. *Something about the book.* No. *Something about Frannie.*

She closed her eyes, concentrating. Frannie had come into the shop asking for the book. When was that? Monday. Molly's day off. Stephanie had been rushed off her feet, unpacking boxes and stocking shelves.

Rick had come into the store and that was when Stephanie had told her to go on a date with him. Frannie had come in while they were in the middle of the argument.

The voices in her head spoke louder. *Frannie asked for the book.* Clara shook her head. *What was wrong with that?* She opened the book, struggling to understand the insistent voices. *Frannie asked for the book.*

Then it dawned on her. Of course. Frannie's words: *I'd like a copy of the Wayne Lester book that just came in.*

Just a few minutes earlier, Stephanie had been stocking the shelves. Clara heard her cousin's voice, as clear as if she were by her side. *We haven't put any new fantasy books out since . . . before Dan closed the store.*

So the big question was — how did Frannie know Wayne Lester's book had arrived?

Before she could think about the consequences of the question, John Halloran's voice scattered her thoughts. "I'm looking for Steve Ratchet's *Searching for a Ghost*. I can't see it on the shelves."

Clara did a quick check on the computer. "It's sold out. We're waiting for new copies now."

"Put one by for me when they come in, please?"

"Of course." She entered his name on the list. "There. We'll let you know when it comes in."

She hoped he'd leave, but he wandered over to the counter, pausing to pick up a publisher's brochure of new titles. "Molly took another day off?"

"No, she called in sick."

His mouth twisted in his unpleasant smile. "She didn't look sick to me."

Clara's fingers paused on the computer's keyboard. "Sorry?"

"I said she didn't look sick to me." He moved closer. "I just saw her a little while ago, heading out of town on the back of a motorbike."

Clara pinched her lips. It wasn't the first

time Molly had lied. In spite of her best efforts to prevent them, the doubts started creeping into her mind. Molly's temper was apparently legendary. She was the last one in the store that night. No sign of a break-in. It was so easy to imagine Ana storming into the stockroom and Molly . . . No. She couldn't go there.

As if reading her thoughts, John spoke again. "No more news on the murder?"

Clara swallowed hard. "Not that I've heard."

He studied the brochure for a moment, then murmured, "Dan was in the store yesterday, asking questions."

She felt a quiver of apprehension, though she wasn't sure why. "In the hardware store?"

"Uh-huh." He looked up, his eyes looking faded behind the lenses of his glasses. "He was in here, too. I guess he went into all the stores around here. He doesn't seem to be having much luck in finding Ana's executioner."

His mouth twitched, and Clara had the uneasy feeling he was trying not to smile. "He will find him eventually," she said, moving a little farther along the counter. "Dan's a good cop. He won't give up until he has the killer behind bars."

John met her gaze. "Let us hope so." He looked down again at the brochure. "Funny thing is, whoever wanted to get rid of her could have just waited a little longer."

The last thing Clara wanted was to prolong the unsettling conversation, but she felt compelled to ask, "Wait? For what?"

"For Ana to move." He looked up again, and edged closer to the counter, sending chills down Clara's arms. "She was looking at property in Portland, you know. She was planning to relocate."

Clara stared at him. "Relocate? When?"

"I don't know." His laugh was completely without humor. "It was only a matter of time, though, and we would all have been rid of her anyway. Rather ironic, don't you think? Though I suppose she could have come back at any time, so whoever killed her did the town a big favor after all." He leaned over the counter, forcing Clara to shrink back. "She got what she deserved. That woman was a she-devil, and good riddance to her, I say."

The venom in his voice scared her, and she cleared her throat. "I'm sorry you feel that way."

"I'm not." To her utter relief, he tucked the brochure in his pocket and strolled toward the door. Opening it, he looked back at her. "I was the last one to see her alive, you know. Lucky me." His high-pitched laugh seemed to hover in the air long after the door had closed behind him.

Thoroughly unnerved, Clara hurried down the aisle to the Nook. Wishing she had a shot of brandy to put in her coffee, she sat down to call Stephanie on her cell phone.

Her cousin answered, sounding frazzled. "The kids just got home from school," she said, "and Olivia's torn another new shirt. She was climbing a tree, of all things. Doesn't she know she's a girl?"

Despite her shattered nerves, Clara laughed. "She'll grow out of it. Just wait until she starts getting interested in boys."

"She's interested in them now. Except she thinks she's one of them. I don't think she'll ever appreciate her feminine side."

"Yes, she will. We did. Eventually."

Stephanie uttered a rueful chuckle. "Yeah, we were little tomboys, weren't we?"

"Totally."

"So what's up?" Stephanie's voice sharpened. "Not trouble at the store, is there?"

"Nope. It's quiet here right now, which is why I'm calling." Clara paused, wondering how best to phrase the question without influencing her cousin's reaction.

"Okay." Now Stephanie sounded curious. "So what's up?"

"Do you remember Frannie asking for Wayne Lester's new book?"

"Of course. A lot of people have been asking for it. He's a popular author. Why?"

"When did you get his books in?"

Stephanie paused, apparently surprised by the question. "They came in on Friday. I unpacked them in the stockroom that afternoon, but I didn't put them out on the shelves right away because I was concentrating on getting out the stock for the back-to-school sale, and then with all the upset of Ana's murder, it was Monday before they ended up on the shelves."

"Do you remember what Frannie said when she asked for the book?"

"Not exactly. Why?"

"She asked for the Wayne Lester book that had just come in."

"She did? But —" She uttered a little gasp. "Oh, my."

"Did you tell Frannie that the book had come in?"

"No, I didn't. Oh, Clara. She couldn't have known unless she was in the stockroom."

Clara let out her breath in a rush. "Exactly."

"We could be wrong, you know. You have to talk to her. Ask her how she knew."

"Me? You know her better than I do. Why can't you talk to her?"

"I'm the ideas person, remember? Besides, you're better at getting stuff out of people than I am. I'm too blunt, and they clam up when I ask questions."

"Like who?"

"Like Tony Manetas, for one. I asked him if he was interested in Aunt Jessie, and he turned beet red and walked away from me."

Clara gasped. "You asked him if he was interested in my *mother?*"

"Well, she was in there the other night when I walked by, and he was leaning over her table, and there was just something in the way he was looking at her, and I thought it was so cute and romantic —"

"Enough! I don't want to know." Clara shook her head. "Back to the Frannie problem."

"The only way we're going to know for sure is to ask her."

"She's not exactly going to come out and say she was in the stockroom —" Clara broke off with a sigh. "Listen to us. We're talking about Frannie, for heaven's sake. She's scared of everyone and everything."

"I know. It seems ridiculous, but we have

to find out for sure before we go to Dan."

"All right." Clara tightened her hold on the phone. "I'll ask her. Somehow."

"Good for you. Call me as soon as you know."

"I can't leave the store until closing. She might have left before then."

"Can't you call her?"

"Of course not. This has to sound casual, like I just thought of it."

"Crap. Then I guess it'll have to wait. Unless I can find someone to watch the kids while I come over there. Too bad Molly is sick; we could have asked her."

Clara fought with her conscience a full five seconds before answering. "Well, don't worry about it. If you can't make it, I'll keep an eye open for Frannie this evening." It wasn't up to her to rat on Molly, she decided. But she'd have a word with that young lady and make sure she didn't goof off and lie about being sick again.

"There's something else," she added, before Stephanie could hang up. "John Halloran was in here."

"Oh?" Stephanie's voice rose a few notches. "Did something happen?"

"Well, not exactly." Clara paused, wondering if once more she was overreacting.

"Tell me!"

"He said he was the last one to see Ana alive."

"He probably was. He was in Jordan's late that night. Frannie told me. They were taking inventory the night Ana was killed. Frannie didn't leave until after nine. She said John came in just before she left." Stephanie paused, then added soberly, "Ana must have been killed shortly after that."

"Was John still there after Frannie left?"

"I don't know. You'll have to ask her." Again the pause. "Even if he was, that doesn't mean he killed Ana."

"I know, but there's just something in the way he says things." Clara shivered. "He can be so weird at times."

"He always was weird. Don't you remember when we were kids, we thought he was an evil wizard?"

"That's because he wouldn't give us samples of candy."

"Yes, but it was the way he wouldn't give it to us. Like he was enjoying the power of denying us what we wanted."

"Well, he told me something else that was kind of odd. He said that Ana was looking at property in Portland and that she was planning on moving there."

"So she must have been planning on selling the store to Roberta anyway."

"Perhaps." Clara sighed. "The more we try to solve this thing, the more complicated it gets."

"I know. No wonder Dan is having such a tough time. Though I do think he still believes Molly killed Ana and is waiting for her to confess."

"By the way, you didn't tell me Dan was in here yesterday. What did he have to say?"

"Not a lot. More questions, mostly asking Molly the same things over and over. I think he's hoping to trip her up."

"Did she tell him she was out with her boyfriend that night?"

"No, I don't think so. I wish she would. I don't like to think of her lying to the cops."

She'd be even more upset if she knew Molly had lied to her, too, Clara thought. She considered, just for a moment, telling Stephanie what John had seen, then once more decided to say nothing. No sense in upsetting her cousin any further.

She hung up, resolving to talk to Molly at the first opportunity.

Stephanie arrived at the bookstore half an hour later, red in the face and obviously rattled. "Mom managed to get off work early," she said, dumping a couple of loaded grocery sacks onto the counter. "I promised her I wouldn't be long."

Now that the moment was at hand, Clara wasn't at all sure she wanted to go through with it. "Frannie's going to be upset, no matter how I phrase the question," she said, keeping her voice low so the customer studying the cookbooks couldn't hear her.

"If she's guilty," Stephanie muttered, "she deserves to be upset. Just be careful. We don't know how she'll react."

Somehow Clara just couldn't imagine being afraid of Frannie. "I'll be right back." She let herself out the door and hurried up the sidewalk to Jordan's front entrance.

Just as she reached the door, Roberta flew out of it, narrowly missing a collision as Clara skipped aside.

"Sorry!" Roberta flapped a hand at her and continued her mad dash across the road, pausing barely long enough to allow a bicyclist to pass before plunging on.

Curious, Clara watched the woman leap across the sidewalk and disappear into Parson's Hardware. Whatever was the reason for her rush, evidently it had something to do with Rick Sanders.

With a let-down feeling washing over her, Clara walked into the spacious interior of Jordan's.

9

Clara found Frannie at the back of the store, fiddling with a screwdriver in the back of a fax machine. She seemed absorbed in her task and jumped when Clara spoke to her.

"Sorry!" Frannie dropped the screwdriver on the counter. "I didn't see you there. Can I get something for you?"

"Er . . ." Clara looked around and spotted an end display.

"Cartridges! That's it! I was . . . ah . . . I wanted to look at . . . ah . . . print cartridges. For my printer." *Of course, idiot.*

Frannie's frown cleared. "Oh, right. They're over there." She nudged her head at the display. "Here, I'll show you."

Following the slender woman across the floor, Clara tried to imagine Frannie slugging Ana over the head with a bust of Poe. Just didn't compute. Still, there was the significant question to be asked, and somehow she had to find a way to pose it.

She pretended to study the cartridges while she sought for a way to open the conversation. "You look pretty efficient with that screwdriver," she said, hoping something significant would come to her.

Frannie's face broke into a smile. "I do all right. When you live alone, you learn to do all kinds of things yourself."

Clara nodded. "I know how that goes. It helps to pass the time. The good thing, though, about living alone is that it gives you plenty of time to read. It's one of my favorite pastimes."

Frannie's face brightened. "Mine, too! I love to read. I have a whole roomful of books I haven't even looked at yet, and still I buy more."

"It can be addictive." She paused, then added casually, "Have you read Wayne Lester's book yet?"

"Oh, yes." Frannie looked positively radiant. "At least, most of it. I haven't quite finished it yet, but it's absolutely fascinating. Have you read his work?"

"No, I . . . haven't. Not yet." She'd been going to say that those kind of books were on the bottom of her reading list. Frannie would not appreciate that. "I'll certainly take a look at it, though."

"It's really good. It's like he knows me personally. He says there are great changes in my future. Quite exciting, really."

Clara squared her shoulders. "That reminds me. There's something I've been meaning to ask you."

"Yes?" Frannie's eyes looked enormous behind her glasses.

"Well, I was just wondering . . . ah . . . when you came in to buy the book. How did you know it was there?"

Frannie looked at her as if she didn't understand the question.

Clara tried again. "I was just wondering how you knew it was in the store. We'd only just put it out on the shelves. We were wondering if you'd seen it advertised somewhere . . . or something."

It was weak, but Frannie seemed okay with it. "Oh, no. Someone told me Wayne's book had come in."

Clara felt goose bumps popping up on her arms. "Really? Who was that?"

Frowning now, Frannie shook her head. "Actually, I don't remember. It was sometime over the weekend, and everyone was upset about Ana. Things are a bit of a blur." Her bottom lip trembled, then she seemed to pull herself together. "It might have been John Halloran. I was in the hardware store

Saturday evening, and we were talking about Ana and he said his stars had predicted a death. Then we got to talking about books on astrology. No, wait."

She paused, her brows furrowed in concentration, while Clara resisted the urge to prod her. Finally, she murmured, "It could have been Rick who told me. He was talking with us, too." She looked up at Clara. "I didn't know he was interested in astrology."

Clara's stomach churned. Funny how Rick's name was mentioned every time the subject of Ana's death came up. The voices started whispering, agreeing with her, warning her. She shut them down.

Frannie peered at her. "Are you all right? You look like you've got the cramps or something."

"Oh, no, I'm fine. It's just the heat." Clara backed away. "I'd better get back to the shop and drink some water."

"What about your cartridges?"

"Oh, that's okay. I'll get them another time." All she wanted to do was get out of there, out into the open, where there were no walls threatening to crush her.

She was almost at the door when Frannie called out after her, "You know, it could have been Roberta who told me. She was there as well. I know it was one of them. Is it important? Was it supposed to be a secret or something?"

Clara shook her head, raised a hand in farewell and dashed out the door.

Stephanie looked up, her eyes wide with expectation as Clara burst into the Raven's Nest. "What is it? Did she confess? What happened?"

Clara stood for a moment, collecting her thoughts. There was no way she was going to admit to Stephanie that she was upset at the mention of Roberta being in Rick's store on Saturday night. After all, it was none of her business what went on between the two of them.

She walked over to the counter and leaned her back against it. Signaling with her eyes and raised eyebrows, she asked a silent question.

"No, there's no customers. You can talk. What is it?" Stephanie rushed over to her. "Tell me!"

"Well, Frannie wasn't in the stockroom I don't think. It could have been John Halloran, though, or Roberta, or . . ."

"Or who?"

She had trouble getting the last name out. "Rick. One of those three told Frannie Saturday evening that the books had arrived. She just can't remember who it was.

She only remembers that sometime over the weekend someone told her."

"Oh, my." Stephanie sagged against the counter.

"We have to tell Dan, I suppose."

"Tell Dan what?" Stephanie shook her head. "We don't know any more than we did yesterday. We've suspected all three of them all along, and Dan has questioned them all already."

"Yes, but he doesn't know about the book thing."

Stephanie opened her mouth to answer, but just then the doorbell chimed, and Frannie hurried into the store. "I've just got a moment," she said, her voice taut with anxiety, "but I remembered who told me about the book. It was Molly. She was leaving the store as I passed by on my way home Friday night, and she said the books had come in and would probably go out on the shelves on Monday." She shook her head. "I don't know why I didn't remember that in the first place. I must be getting old."

Limp with relief, Clara could have hugged her. Stephanie assured the anxious woman that there was no problem with the books and that they were just curious, that's all, and after a few more reassuring words, Frannie nodded and darted off.

"Well, that's that." Stephanie sounded defeated as she returned to the counter. "We're back to square one. Thank goodness we didn't go to Dan with this. We'd have looked like fools."

"Not to mention putting suspicion on three innocent people."

"We don't know that they're innocent. All we know is that none of them have any incriminating evidence against them. It doesn't mean one of them didn't kill Ana." Stephanie sent her an accusing look. "I don't suppose you've had any luck with the Quinn Sense?"

Clara shrugged. "I told you it was unpredictable and unreliable. It comes and goes but so far hasn't told me anything useful."

"You used to be able to see into the future *and* interpret dreams."

"Not all the time."

"A lot of the time. You could always tell when someone was lying. I remember when Tommy Ridgeworth told you he couldn't meet you that night because his car broke down. You marched into the movie theater, right up to where he was sitting with Veronica Kassell, and dumped a whole carton of soda and ice on his head."

Clara had to smile at the memory. "So what are you suggesting? That I go ask all three of our suspects if they've murdered Ana and hope I can tell if they're lying?"

"No, of course not."

"Good, because I can tell you from past experience, the Sense doesn't always come through for me, usually when I need it the most."

Stephanie narrowed her eyes. "It let you down badly in New York, didn't it?"

Clara turned away and her voice was short when she answered.

"Yes. It did."

"Want to talk about it?"

Normally she would have changed the subject, but she was feeling vulnerable and the urge to share the past with her cousin was too strong to ignore. "It's not unique. I met someone I thought I wanted to marry."

"That's the guy you never wanted to talk about when you came home to visit?"

"Yes." Clara ran a finger along the counter to wipe away imaginary dust. "I guess somewhere deep inside I knew something was wrong. I just didn't want to admit it. I wanted to be sure of him before I told anyone about him."

"What happened?"

Clara waited until she could trust her voice before answering. "He forgot to mention there was someone else in the picture."

"Oh, God. And you couldn't tell he was lying to you?"

"No, I couldn't." Clara clenched her fist on the counter.

"That was the problem. I relied so much on the stupid Sense thing that I'd stopped listening to my own instincts. Now I'm not even sure I have instincts anymore."

"Of course you do. You just have to learn to believe in them again." Stephanie threw her arms around her and hugged her tight. "Men can be such monsters. I'm so lucky to have George."

"Yes, you are." Clara blinked hard. "Hang on to him. Those kind don't come along every day."

"No wonder you find it so hard to trust." Stephanie let her go as the doorbell jangled again. "You'll find the right man. He's out there somewhere. You just have to find him."

"Can I help?"

The familiar voice sent a rush of blood to Clara's cheeks.

She turned to face Rick Sanders, her gaze skidding past his face and resting somewhere over by the door.

Stephanie made matters worse by saying lightly, "I don't know. Can you?"

"Just say the word, and I'm your man." He looked at Clara. "Lose your dog? Cat?

Not a child, I hope?"

Clara sent a furious glance at her cousin before saying tightly, "We didn't lose anything. We were just talking, that's all." She still couldn't look at him, uncertain exactly how much he'd overheard.

"Well, I'd better get going." Stephanie picked up the grocery sacks and headed for the door. "I'll see you in the morning, Clara. Don't forget your promise, now."

By the time Clara realized what she meant, she had disappeared into the street.

The promise. Her idiot cousin still thought she'd make another date with Rick to find out if he had an alibi. Even after she'd told her she'd had lunch with him and couldn't find out anything. Stephanie being Stephanie, however, couldn't leave it there. Oh, no. She'd insisted that Clara try again. Well, Clara wasn't about to —

"Was it something I said?"

Rick's voice jerked her out of her thoughts. "Sorry?"

"You had such a fierce look on your face I thought you must be mad at me for something."

"Oh, no, sorry. I was thinking about something else." She made an effort to smile at him. "Can I get you something?"

"Maybe." He sauntered over to the cookbook shelves and ran a finger along the back of the books. "How about a slice of pepperoni pizza?"

"Pizza?" She stared down the aisle in the direction of the Nook, wondering if Stephanie kept pizza somewhere she didn't know about.

"Tonight." He turned to look at her. "At the Pizza Parlor. That's if your mother hasn't prepared dinner for you already."

She hesitated just a tad too long. He nodded, as if to confirm something to himself. "Too much, too soon, right?"

Feeling like a prize idiot, she said quickly, "No, it's just —"

He held up his hand as he strode toward the door. "It's okay. Really. I understand." He was gone before she could answer.

Cursing under her breath, Clara watched him walk across the street and into his store. That was twice she'd rejected him.

She could hardly tell him that if and when she decided to go out with him — and it was a big if — she wanted it to be a real date, and not an excuse for an inquisition.

There was also the possibility that he'd been involved in Ana's murder. Though the longer she was around him, the more certain she felt that he had nothing to do with it.

Last, and certainly not least, there was the

question of his connection with Roberta Prince. Until all that was cleared up, she didn't feel comfortable having any kind of relationship with him, casual or otherwise.

Having decided on that, she marched back to the Nook, wishing she didn't keep having the persistent feeling that somehow she was missing something.

Soon after that she had a little rush of customers, and she welcomed them, thankful to have something to take her mind off her problems. She had just watched the last one walk out the door when one of her problems turned up on the doorstep.

Roberta Prince charged into the store as if she were riding into battle. Ignoring Clara behind the counter, she rushed over to the display of cookbooks and started picking them up, glancing at the cover before throwing each one aside to reach for another.

Unable to stand it any longer, Clara hurried over to her. "Were you looking for anything in particular? Perhaps I can help?"

Roberta's glance flicked over her. "I don't really know what I'm looking for. Rick said you have some excellent cookbooks, and I wanted to see for myself."

Did he, really? Clara ignored the voice. "There's a lot to choose from there. Most of them are specialized, but if you're looking for a general variety of dishes, this one is very extensive."

She picked up the heavy tome, but Roberta shook her head. "I think something a little more Italian. Rick told me he's fond of Italian cooking."

Clara's fingers tightened on the book, and she slowly set it down. "Yes, so I heard."

Roberta turned to face her, her sharp eyes probing Clara's face. "He doesn't know it yet," she said, her voice oozing confidence, "but Rick Sanders is going to be my next husband. I'm sure enough of that to have put a considerable amount of my divorce settlement into that dismal stationer's next door. It gives me the golden opportunity to be in his face every day, and trust me, eventually I'll wear him down."

She walked off, leaving Clara standing there with her jaw hanging open. Reaching the door, she turned around, and Clara clapped her mouth shut. "Believe me," Roberta added, "I'll get what I want. I always do." Her smile reminded Clara of the Cheshire cat's — all teeth and no substance.

She waited until Roberta had closed the door behind her, then let out an explosive "Bitch!" Reaching for the phone, she stabbed out Stephanie's number and waited impatiently for her cousin to answer.

Just before the line went to voice mail, Stephanie snapped an irritated "Hello?"

"It's me." Clara drew a deep breath. "Is this a bad time?"

"Yes . . . No . . . Oh, it's okay. What's up?"

"Roberta was just in here."

"Oh?" Stephanie paused, then added, "Did something happen?"

"Not exactly." Clara was beginning to wish she hadn't called. It all sounded a bit juvenile now that she thought about it.

"So why are you calling?"

"I thought you'd like to know the real reason Roberta wanted Ana's store."

"No way! She told you? What is it?"

"She wants Rick Sanders."

There was a short spell of silence, then Stephanie said cautiously, "You mean Rick's store?"

"No, I mean Rick." Clara repeated Roberta's exact words. "That . . . *woman* made an excuse to come in here to warn me he was off-limits. Like I care."

"You sound like you care."

"Well, I don't. I just didn't like the way she spoke to me. What gives her the idea that I'm interested in him, anyway?"

"She must have seen you together."

Clara frowned. "What does that mean?"

171

"Well, you do get all twittery when you're around him."

"Twittery? Is that even a word?"

"I think so. I think I read it somewhere. Anyway, it's *my* word."

Clara straightened her back. "I do not get *twittery* or anything else around Rick Sanders. I'm not in the least bit interested in him, and I couldn't care less if he and Roberta Prince got married and had a ton of babies. Just as long as they don't bring them all in here."

Stephanie giggled. "Somehow the idea of Roberta Prince being the mother of a baker's dozen seems ludicrous."

"Yes, well, she certainly needn't worry about me. As far as I'm concerned, she can keep Rick Sanders all to herself and good luck to them both."

"Say that often enough and you'll start to believe —" Stephanie broke off with a groan. Clara could hear her yelling from a distance, "Livvy? *Olivia!* Put the cat down! This minute! I mean right *now!*" Her voice sounded closer again when she added, "I've got to go. Olivia is trying to put Michael's baby shoes on the cat. One of them is going to end up getting hurt. Don't worry about Roberta. She's harmless, and Rick is a big guy. He can take care of himself."

She hung up, leaving Clara no chance to emphasize her complete indifference to the whole thing.

Who are you kidding?

"Shut up!" she said out loud and went back to the Nook for another cup of coffee.

10

As Clara left the Raven's Nest that night, she saw Frannie wheeling her bike across the sidewalk. She called out to her, and Frannie answered with a wave, hesitated, then turned and walked toward her, still pushing her bike.

"You might like to know," she said, when she got close enough for Clara to hear her, "Roberta is putting the print cartridges on sale this weekend. Ten percent off."

Touched by the gesture, Clara smiled. "Thanks for letting me know." She eyed the bike. "You don't ride that in bad weather, do you?"

Frannie laughed. "Not if it's snowing or icy, no. Then I usually walk."

"You don't have a car?"

"Oh, I have one. I just don't drive it much." She glanced across the street. "There's John leaving. He's late tonight. He usually leaves around seven."

Clara hesitated, then decided to seize the opportunity. "He was in Jordan's late the night Ana died, wasn't he?"

Frannie gave her a sharp glance. "Yes, he came in for some hanging files. He's one of our best customers."

"That's nice." Clara paused, wondering how to phrase the question, then figured she might as well come right out and ask.

"Do you remember if he was still there when you left?"

"No, I don't remember. I told Dan I couldn't remember. I think he was, but he might not have been." She was backing away as she spoke, glancing down the road to make sure it was clear before wheeling her bike out into the road. "I wish people wouldn't keep asking me questions. I want to forget what happened. All these questions upset me."

Following her, Clara called out, "I'm sorry. It's just that he told me he was the last one to see Ana alive. I was just wondering how he knew that, that's all."

"I don't know, and I don't want to know." Frannie hopped on her bike and started pedaling furiously down the road. "No more questions, all right?"

Her voice floated back up the hill just as the whispering started in Clara's head. *Fran-*

175

nie is afraid of something. Or someone.

Did she know more than she was telling everyone? Clara frowned as she walked rapidly down the hill to the parking lot.

Was it possible Frannie knew for certain who had killed Ana and was too afraid to tell anyone? If so, she could be in danger. Whoever killed Ana would probably have no hesitation in killing anyone else who got in his way. Especially someone as vulnerable as Frannie.

The idea worried her, so much so that the moment she got to the Raven's Nest the next day, she took Stephanie to the stockroom, leaving Molly to take care of the counter.

"I think we should mention it to Dan," she said, when she'd finished telling her cousin about her conversation with Frannie. "She might need protection."

"Dan's shorthanded as it is. He probably won't assign someone to protect her until he's sure there's something to protect her from," Stephanie declared. "You know Frannie. She's afraid of her own shadow. Whatever she knows, she's not going to tell Dan or she would have done so by now." She peered up at Clara. "How do you know she's in danger, anyway?"

"I don't. Not really." Clara pretended to

176

be examining a box of books. "It's just a feeling, that's all."

"Aha! The Quinn Sense!" Stephanie looked excited. "You've been hearing it, haven't you?"

"Just a whisper now and then. Nothing major."

"But it told you Frannie is in danger."

"No, that was purely a guess on my part. It's just that she seems so afraid every time we mention the murder. I just have a feeling that she knows more than she's willing to admit. She might even know something incriminating. If so, the killer will eventually find out she knows and might decide to get rid of her."

Stephanie shivered. "Stop. You're creeping me out."

"Good. Then don't you think it's time we had a talk with Dan?"

"I guess." She looked hopeful. "Why don't you call in at the station and talk to him? I can hang on here for another hour or so."

Clara ignored the little flip of anxiety. "I thought we might go together."

"Well, you know I would, but I still have a ton of books to shelve and —"

"Never mind. I'll go." Clara left before she vented her frustration on her cousin. She wasn't about to admit, even to herself, that the reason for her bad mood could be her conversation with Roberta Prince the night before.

It didn't help to see Rick standing outside his store, talking to John Halloran. She was beginning to wish she'd never agreed to help Stephanie in the bookstore. She'd come home to Finn's Harbor for some peace and quiet, and the last thing she needed was this kind of aggravation.

She was about to head down the hill to the police station when she spotted Dan's car outside Jordan's. Deciding to wait for him, she pretended to study the bookstore's windows.

Stephanie had draped filmy, multicolored gauze behind the displays, creating a somewhat eerie effect that was heightened by a crystal ball perched on a spindly table in the center of the window.

Among the gauze were scattered tiny crystals and sequins. They caught the light and twinkled as a draft slowly swayed the drapes back and forth. Clara tilted her head to better enjoy the spectacle and out of the corner of her eye caught sight of Dan leaving the stationer's.

She hurried over to him, still conscious of Rick talking on the sidewalk across the street.

Dan greeted her with a gruff "How're you doing?"

"Fine, thanks." She glanced at the stationer's but couldn't see anyone inside. "Could I have a quick word with you?"

"Sure." His shrewd gaze raked her face. "You wanna talk here or in the car?"

She hesitated, then said quickly, "In the car if that's okay."

For answer he opened the door of the passenger side and waited for her to slide in.

She shivered as the door shut with a thud. It was the first time she'd been inside a cop car. There seemed to be an awful lot of gadgets. She was intrigued to notice that instead of an armrest, the car was fitted with a swivel mount to hold a laptop computer.

Dan climbed in the other side of her and closed the door.

He must have noticed her apprehension, as he said quietly, "Don't let this thing scare you. It's just a car."

Conscious of the steel mesh wall behind her, she gave him a weak grin. "Then why does it feel like I'm on my way to prison?"

"It's designed to scare the heck out of lawbreakers." He jerked a thumb over his shoulder. "Notice that the roof back there is lower?"

She twisted her head to look. "Why's that?"

"It's so a perp doesn't have much room to lunge about, but it's also a bit threatening to have to sit there hunched down like that. Takes some of the pep out of 'em."

"I never thought about that."

"See this?" He reached up and switched on the interior lights. Then he switched them again and they turned from white to red. "That's so the lights don't mess with your night vision. It helps when you have to read a driver's license at night."

Aware that he was trying to put her at ease, she nodded. "That makes sense."

He gave her another of his long looks. "So, little lady, what did you want to talk to me about?"

Now that she was actually talking to him, she began to worry that her overactive imagination was blowing everything out of proportion. Still, she could hardly back out now. "This may be nothing at all," she began, "but I thought I should mention it, anyway."

Dan nodded, his eyes watchful. "Go on."

"It's about Frannie." She hesitated, then blurted out in a rush, "I think she knows something about the murder, and she's afraid to tell anyone."

Dan's expression remained exactly the same. Not even a muscle twitch. "What makes you think that?"

Clara shifted on her seat. "It's just that every time anyone mentions anything about the murder, Frannie acts kind of terrified, as if she's afraid to talk about it."

Dan seemed to think that one over. "Well," he said at last, "I've talked to her a couple of times, and I'm pretty sure she would have told me if she'd known who was responsible. I reckon Frannie is the kind of woman who gets spooked pretty darn quick, and she's shook up real bad over Ana getting killed like that. She just doesn't like talking about it, I guess. Some people would rather bury their heads in the sand than face what's real. Frannie's the type who thinks if she pretends it didn't happen, then it never did."

Don't listen to him.

The voice came from nowhere, so clear it made her jump. She felt an urgent need to get out of that car, away from all the gadgets and mesh wall and threatening roof.

"Okay, then I won't worry about her." She reached for the handle and pushed open the door. "Thanks for listening. Sorry if I wasted your time."

"It's never a waste of time to spend a pleasant moment or two with a pretty lady."

181

Dan's smile was genuine, and she grinned back at him. "Flattery will get you everywhere." She closed the door and watched him drive off. Just before she turned to go back into the Raven's Nest, she glanced across the street.

Both Rick and John Halloran stood staring at her.

She waved at them and didn't wait to see if they waved back.

Stephanie and Molly looked up as she walked into the bookstore. "That was quick," Stephanie said, glancing at the clock on the wall. "Did you get to see Dan?"

"I saw him come out of Jordan's, so I talked to him in his car."

"Oh, man," Molly said, shivering. "I had to ride in it when he took me to the station. It's so creepy."

Knowing how much worse it must have been in the backseat, Clara felt bad for her.

"So, what did he say?" Stephanie demanded.

"Not a lot." For some reason, Clara felt uncomfortable talking about it in front of Molly.

Stephanie didn't seem to have any qualms about it. "Did you tell him you thought Frannie might be in danger?"

Molly gasped. "Is she? From what?"

"We don't know," Clara said, giving Stephanie what she hoped was a meaningful look. "She just acts scared, and I thought she might be frightened of something. Or someone."

Molly looked disappointed. "Frannie is always scared of something."

"That's what Dan said." Clara stowed her purse under the counter. "Anyway, I feel better about it now. Did you guys know that a police car's inside lights can be turned to red at night?"

She went on to explain why, thankful for having successfully changed the subject. For no matter what Dan said, she couldn't shake the idea that Frannie knew something about the murder and was too afraid to tell anyone. Maybe Frannie was right in suspecting Roberta. If so, they were up against a formidable foe.

Apparently the Sense agreed with her, as later that night, just as she was leaving, the word *danger* kept repeating itself over and over in her mind.

The day had been unusually cool for September, and the evening breeze carried a promise of fall as it drifted in from the ocean. The sun had already set, leaving just a faint, thin line of purple above the horizon. Even as she watched, that, too, disappeared, and the sea turned black.

As she walked down the hill, she could see a faint circle of mist shrouding each of the streetlamps. A sure sign that the summer was dying. Soon the nights would be crisp and cool, and the days just pleasantly warm.

It was her favorite time of the year, especially in Finn's Harbor, when the trees were bathed in red and gold, painting the hills with glorious color.

Immersed in anticipation of the approaching holidays, she was smiling as she walked across the parking lot to her car. At the far end she saw a red pickup turn onto the street, its taillights eventually vanishing into the darkness.

It made her think of Rick, and she wondered if he'd gone to the Pizza Parlor the night before. Maybe he'd taken Roberta.

Angry with herself, she dragged the car door open and flung herself onto the seat. *Forget Rick.*

Good advice, but it was a little tough to do that when he was in her face every day. Roberta's voice seemed to ring in her ears. *It gives me the golden opportunity to be in his face every day, and trust me, eventually I'll wear him down.*

Clara shook her head as she turned the

key in the ignition.

She had no doubt at all that Roberta would succeed. Any woman who had gone to such great lengths to get her man wouldn't give up easily. She wasn't sure whom to feel sorry for the most, Rick or herself.

There she went again. Irritated, she slammed the car into reverse and shot out of the parking space, only to be brought up short by the thick hedge behind her. Shaken, she gave herself a mental shake. *Calm down.* The last thing she wanted to do was wrap the car around a lamppost.

She pushed the gear into drive and pulled out of the parking lot onto an empty street. Her headlights lit up the sidewalk as she started down the hill toward the harbor. She was almost at the bottom, gathering speed, when a cat darted across the road in front of her.

Her foot automatically smacked down on the brake pedal, and she braced for the screeching halt. The next moment, panic hit her full force. She was still racing down the hill.

Clinging to the steering wheel, she pummeled the brake over and over, while the car headed straight for the harbor wall and the ocean beyond.

Her first thought was that she was about to die. Hot on the heels of that thought came the determined vow to live, no matter what it took.

She shoved the gear into park and shut off the engine. The emergency brake had no affect as she hurtled downward, her hand on the horn. Frantically she looked right and left, hoping to see something that would bring her car to a halt with a reasonable hope of surviving the impact.

Stores whizzed past her on both sides at an alarming speed.

Her only hope, she decided, was the vacant lot on the corner of Main and Harbor. It was coming up fast on her right. Praying as she'd never prayed before, she spun the wheel.

The car bucked and swerved, and for a terrifying moment she thought it would turn over. Then the tires grabbed and she shot over the curb, flying through the air for several feet before she bounced down hard on the uneven surface.

It was open ground before her and flat, but bordered on two sides by brick buildings. She had little room to maneuver, and she turned the wheel hard, hoping to keep the car moving in a circle until it slowed down.

She almost made it. The rear end of the car just nicked the corner of a building, sending her fishtailing across the lot. She saw another wall coming at her and threw both her arms in front of her face.

The last thing she remembered was the awful sound of tearing metal and somewhere in the distance the piercing shriek of brakes. Then nothing.

Stephanie finished putting the last dish away in the dishwasher and pulled a sheet off the paper-towel holder to dry her hands. Glancing at her watch, she frowned, then called out to George in the living room. "Honey? What's the time?"

The babble of voices on the TV faded to a quiet hum. George's tired voice answered her. "What was that?"

"I said, what's the time?" Stephanie poked her head into the living room, where her husband sat sprawled on the couch. "My watch says ten fifteen, but it can't be that late, can it?"

"I don't see why not." George nodded at the mantelpiece. "Ten fifteen on the dot. Time marches on."

"That's weird."

"That time marches on or that you can't keep track of it?"

"Very funny." She made a face at him and walked over to sit down next to him. "It's just that Clara usually calls me when she gets home to let me know everything's okay at the shop."

"Well, maybe she's not home yet."

"Then where would she be?"

"Why are you asking me? I'm not her keeper."

She stirred uneasily, a niggling worry beginning to attack her mind. In the old days, before Clara moved to New York, they could usually sense when one or the other was in trouble.

Clara's intuition was much stronger than hers, of course, but at least where Clara was concerned, she must have inherited just a slight twinge of the Quinn Sense. Or maybe it was just a common old sixth sense, but whatever it was, right now she could feel it, throbbing in the back of her head.

"I'm going to call her," she said, jumping to her feet so suddenly that George jerked his head back with a grunt of surprise.

"What if she's in bed?" He pushed himself upright on the couch, concern written all over his face.

"Then she'll have to wake up to answer." Stephanie found her cell phone on the kitchen counter and rapidly thumbed out her cousin's number.

With the phone pressed to her ear, she walked back into the living room. "She's not answering. Something's wrong."

"Maybe she's too tired to answer."

"She always answers me."

"She could be on a date and . . . ah . . . occupied."

Stephanie gave him a scathing look. "We're talking about *Clara* here. Even if she did go on a date, which I seriously doubt, she wouldn't be doing *that* on the first night."

George shrugged. "Nowadays most people do *that* on the first night."

"And how would you happen to know that?"

"I watch TV, read the newspapers, and go on the Internet."

Too distracted to argue with him, Stephanie stabbed out another number on her cell phone.

"I hope you're not calling the police," George said, sounding alarmed.

"I'm calling Aunt Jessie. She can at least tell me if Clara's home." Stephanie waited, heart pounding, while the line buzzed in her ear. "She's not there, either," she said at last as she snapped her phone shut.

"They're probably out somewhere together," George said, reaching for the remote.

Stephanie rolled her eyes at the ceiling, then rushed out of the room.

George called out after her. "Where are you going?"

"I'm going over there." She dragged her jacket from the hall closet and struggled into it. "Something's wrong. I know it. I have to find out if she's okay."

George appeared in the doorway, his face set in a stern scowl that warned her of a forthcoming argument. "I don't want you going out there tonight. Just because Clara doesn't answer her phone doesn't have to mean she's in some kind of dire situation. She won't thank you for barging in on her if she doesn't feel like talking to you."

Stephanie headed for the front door. "May I remind you," she said over her shoulder, "that just a few days ago Ana Jordan was clubbed to death in my stockroom. Don't tell me I'm overreacting. There's a killer out there somewhere, and Clara has been asking questions and talking to the police. I'd say there's plenty to worry about when she doesn't answer her phone."

"Steph, wait a minute." George started toward her, but just then her cell phone sang out, making her jump.

"There she is now," George said, his voice heavy with relief.

He turned away from her and went back into the living room as she spoke into the phone. "Clara? Is that you?"

Dan's voice answered her, filling her with dread. "Stephanie? Sorry to call so late, but I thought you ought to know. It's about Clara. I'm afraid she's been involved in an accident."

Stephanie uttered a desperate little cry that brought George back to the door.

"Who is it? Is it Clara? What's going on?"

"She's been in an accident." Stephanie fought back tears as she spoke into the phone again. "Dan? What happened? Is she all right?"

Tears already falling, she waited for his reply, praying that he wouldn't tell her Clara had been badly hurt. Or worse.

11

She had to be dreaming. If so, it was a painful dream. Her head felt like it was being split in two by a sledgehammer. Both her knees were held tight in some kind of vice that squeezed so hard the pain was almost unbearable. To make matters worse, Rick Sanders had appeared in her dream.

He sat beside her, holding her hand. She tried to snatch it away, but for some reason her arm didn't seem to be working. Whatever she was lying on rumbled and shook beneath her, and there was something covering her nose and mouth.

She lifted her free hand to touch it and heard someone say, "She's coming around."

"Thank God," Rick muttered, and squeezed her fingers.

She opened her mouth to tell him to go away, but the only sound she could make was a soft moan.

"The meds will kick in soon," someone

said, and a boyish face above a white coat smiled down at her.

She rolled her gaze back to Rick's face. He looked awful. His hair was all mussed, and he had a deep scratch down one side of his face. She wanted to ask him what had happened to him, but her head hurt too much to even try to speak.

"Hi," he said, with a lopsided smile. "Welcome back."

She was beginning to remember. The car careening down the hill with no way to stop it. She was sure she was going to die.

But it must have stopped because here she was. Unless she had died and this was in the next world.

No, that couldn't be. For one thing she hurt too much. Dead people couldn't hurt, could they? Then there was Rick. If she was dead, then he was, too, because she could definitely feel the pressure of his hand. And he was talking to her.

Only his voice was coming from a long way off, and she couldn't . . . quite . . . understand . . .

She opened her eyes with a jerk that hurt her head again. She couldn't feel Rick's hand anymore.

The bed beneath her had stopped rumbling and rolling, and now she could see the room. Pale green walls, white ceiling with a bright light above her. Curtains pulled around her, and high bars on either side of her. A needle was attached to her arm, fastened there with white tape, and a tube led up to a bottle that steadily dripped from a stand above her head.

She was in a hospital.

She turned her head, wincing as pain sliced across her forehead and started throbbing behind her eyes. There was a gap in the curtains near the foot of the bed. Someone sat on a chair outside. She could just see a pair of jeans and brown boots.

She tried out her voice. "Hello?"

It sounded weak and raw, as if she had a bad cold. Whoever was outside had heard it, though. The jeans got up and Rick Sanders poked his head inside the curtain.

"Hi there, Sleeping Beauty." He walked over to the bed and stood smiling down at her. "How's the headache?"

She frowned. Even that hurt and she quickly straightened out her forehead. "How'd you know my head aches?"

"The doc said you've got a slight concussion." He sat down on a chair close by. "Other than that, you got away with a few bruises. You probably won't feel like dancing a tango for a while, though."

"Just as well, since I've got two left feet." She peered at him through a bright haze that hurt her eyes. "What happened to me?"

His grin disappeared. "Your brakes went out. You made a rather spectacular entrance onto a vacant lot and tried to turn it into a racetrack."

Now she remembered. "I thought I was going to die."

"So did I."

The stark look on his face surprised her. "You saw it?"

"I'd stopped off at the post office to mail some bills, and I heard your horn. I saw a little crowd gathering at the corner of Main and I got there just in time to see you charging across the lot. You hit the wall pretty hard. I wasn't sure what I'd find when I got to your car."

She actually saw him shudder. "I don't remember much after that."

He seemed to make an effort to collect his thoughts. "I was there ahead of the crowd and called Emergency for an ambulance. The whole front of your car was crushed. It's totaled, by the way."

A wave of nausea took her by surprise, and she started pulling in deep breaths. Rick didn't seem to notice, as he went on talking in a voice drained of emotion. "I couldn't open the door, but I could see you half buried in your air bag. I smashed the window because I was afraid you'd suffocate, but the medics got there pretty fast, and they got the door open."

She remembered waking up in the ambulance. "You rode with me to the hospital."

"Yep." Now he looked worried. "I . . . er . . . had to tell the medics a lie. They weren't too excited about me riding with them."

"A lie?"

"Yeah. I told them we were engaged."

"You *what?*" She started to lift her head, but the pain sliced behind her eyes, and she lay back with a groan.

"Hey, I'm sorry. It was the only way I could get them to take me. You kept insisting you didn't want them to call anyone, and I just thought you might feel better if you saw a familiar face when you woke up."

She waited for the agony to subside before opening her eyes.

"You do realize that the news will be all over town by morning? That my *mother* will think I'm sleeping with you? What were you *thinking?*"

"Sorry," he said again, really sounding it this time. "I guess I didn't stop to think. You looked so defenseless lying there, and I

196

just wanted to be there when you woke up. I'll explain everything to everyone. I promise."

The curtain swished aside at that moment and a woman in a nurse's uniform swept in bearing a tray. "You'll have to leave," she said to Rick. "We've got things to do."

Rick stood and reached for Clara's hand. "Have a good night. I'll see you tomorrow."

She met his gaze and held it. "Please, don't tell anyone. I'll call my family myself later."

"Got it." He gave her hand a squeeze, nodded at the nurse and disappeared through the curtain.

The nurse looked after him and shook her head. "Such a charmer, that one. It's hard to trust a charmer."

Clara was inclined to agree.

"The police chief is outside," the nurse added, unrolling the blood pressure monitor. "He wants a word with you when we're done here. I told him it would be okay if you felt up to it."

Clara gave her a weak nod. She couldn't imagine why Dan would want to talk to her now. She could only hope she wasn't in any trouble.

"I told you something was wrong. I *told*

you!" Tears streaming down her face, Stephanie pummeled George's arm as they raced down the highway.

"Hey! Quit that or you'll be sending us both to the hospital."

Stephanie just cried harder, sobbing into a wad of tissues until they were soaking wet.

"Come on, Steph." George released one of his hands from the wheel to give her a quick hug. "Dan said she wasn't badly hurt. Just cuts and bruises, that's all."

"And a c-concussion."

"A slight concussion, which is why they're keeping her in the hospital overnight for observation."

"Oh, George. I should have been with her when she got there. Why did Dan wait so long to call me?"

"He said Clara didn't want him to call anyone. She didn't want to upset everyone. She's probably mad at him right now for calling you." George swept onto the off-ramp and turned the corner.

"Well, I'm glad he did." Stephanie sniffed and blew her nose on the soggy tissues. "Thank goodness Mom was able to come over and watch the kids, or we would have had to bring them, too."

"That would have been fun," George said, cursing as a red light forced him to a stop.

"Did Dan say what happened?" Stephanie rubbed her eyes with the back of her hand. "I don't remember much after you took the phone from me. I think I was in shock or something."

"You were bawling so hard you couldn't hear anything Dan was saying." George sent her a look of concern. "You're not going to start again, are you?"

She managed a weak "No."

"Good. It won't do Clara much good to see you like this."

"So tell me what happened." She hunted for dry tissues while he told her the few details Dan had told him. "Dan said it could have been a lot worse. Apparently, Clara did everything right and kept her head."

"Clara always keeps her head. I wish I could be like her."

George smiled. "Well, kitten, I'm glad you're not. I happen to like you just the way you are."

"Oh, George. You always know the right thing to say." Warmed by his words, she blew her nose for the last time. She wouldn't feel better until she had actually seen for herself that her cousin was okay, but she had to admit, she was beginning to feel a little less devastated. At least Clara hadn't been clubbed over the head by a murderous villain. Now that would really have been something to worry about.

Dan met them in the foyer when they arrived at the hospital, his expression even more grave than usual.

At first, Stephanie thought that Clara was more badly hurt than Dan had told her, but she relaxed a bit when Dan assured her that Clara was sleeping, and the doctor expected to release her the next morning.

"I would like a word with you, though, before you go in there." Dan glanced at the nurse's station. "That's if they let you go in."

"Just let them try and stop me." Stephanie sent a fierce glance at the nurse behind the desk.

Dan's face softened a little, though he stopped short of an actual smile. "Well, it's about Clara's car. I had Tim check it out before it was towed away." He shifted his weight and glanced around the foyer as if making sure he wouldn't be overheard. "The thing is, it looks as if someone might have cut the brake lines. We can't say for sure at this point, but if we're right, someone out there wanted Clara to wreck her car."

Stephanie thrust a hand over her mouth to prevent her cry of dismay, while George uttered a grunt of disbelief. "Who in hell would want to do that?"

Dan shrugged. "I was hoping you guys might be able to help with that. You know of anyone who might want to hurt her?"

Stephanie tried to look innocent while she struggled with indecision. If she told Dan that Ana's murderer was probably responsible for the wreck, then she'd have to admit they were trying to track him down. The last thing she wanted was to get them both in trouble for interfering in police business.

On the other hand, she couldn't just ignore the fact that Clara was in danger and Dan should know about it. Before she could say anything, however, a piercing cry erupted from the doorway.

Jessie Quinn tottered toward them on her skinny high heels, her makeup overpowering on her white face. "My baby! Where is she? I must see her right now!"

Stephanie darted over to her and grabbed her arm. "She's all right, Aunt Jess. Just a slight concussion. She's sleeping and —"

Jessie's howling drowned out her words. Behind her, the nurse called out, "Ma'am? Could you please keep it down?"

"Come on," Stephanie said, dragging on her aunt's arm. "We'll go to the waiting room and wait for the doctor. George? Ask the nurse to send Clara's doctor in when he's got time."

"That could take *hours*," Jessie wailed.

"I'm sure it won't." Stephanie rolled her eyes at Dan, and he beckoned her over.

Leaving Jessie's side for a moment, Stephanie hurried over to him.

"Don't repeat any of what I said to anyone," Dan said quietly. "I'll talk to you both tomorrow." He raised a hand to George and crossed the foyer to the door.

"What's he doing here?" Jessie demanded, as she watched Dan leave. "Clara wasn't doing anything wrong, was she?"

"No, of course not." Stephanie led the way to the waiting room, wishing she hadn't eaten pizza for dinner. It wasn't sitting too well on her stomach.

Jessie refused her offer to get coffee and sat rocking back and forth, complaining about car manufacturers and the shoddy work they put out. "She just bought that car two months ago, when she knew she was moving back here," she said, dabbing at her red-rimmed eyes. "Now the brakes fail? Disgusting. Those people should be imprisoned for life."

Stephanie agreed with her and assured her over and over again that Clara was going to be fine and would be coming home the next day. It wasn't until the doctor arrived and repeated the same news that Jessie finally stopped gnawing on her nails and appeared to accept the fact that her daughter was not on her deathbed.

Stephanie could find little relief in that, however. Someone had tried to kill Clara. The same someone, presumably, who had killed Ana. It was getting uncomfortably obvious that neither of them would be safe until the killer was caught and put away. So far, it seemed unlikely that would be any time soon.

It was not a comforting thought.

Clara woke up with a start, her mind still reeling from the frightening dream. It was dark in her cubicle, with just a dim light filtering through the curtains. Hushed voices murmuring farther down the ward and the soft squeak of wheels told her the hospital staff were nearby.

It was comforting to a degree, but she couldn't shake off the fear she'd felt when Dan had told her someone had cut the brake lines of her car. *Someone wanted her dead.*

She turned over, wincing as once more pain stabbed her in the forehead. She had to be getting close to Ana's killer, though she wished she knew whatever it was the killer thought she knew. She tried to focus on the last few days, going over everything she could remember.

John Halloran and his sinister comments, with so much reason to hate Ana. Molly's lies. Roberta Prince and her obsession with Rick Sanders. Rick himself — agreeable and just a little intriguing. Could she trust him? She wanted to, but —

The flash of memory hit her hard enough to take her breath away. She started to sit up, but the pain sent her head back on the pillow. The parking lot the night before. The red pickup taking off in the dark, just before she'd reached her car.

The same red pickup that had followed her out of the parking lot in Sealwich Bay, with Rick behind the wheel? What was it he'd said last night?

I'd stopped off at the post office to mail some bills, and I heard your horn.

Coincidence? Or had he been waiting for her at the bottom of the hill? Waiting to see if his little hatchet job had worked?

No! You're on the wrong track!

She closed her eyes. Oh, how she wanted to believe that. Was it the Sense telling her or her own instincts? How could she tell the difference anymore?

The curtain swished aside, making her

jump. The pleasant face of the doctor who'd treated her the night before smiled down at her. "Ah, you're awake. How do you feel? How's the headache?"

"Almost gone." She would have told him that no matter how bad it was. She wanted out of there. Even her mother's house seemed like a sanctuary right then.

"Good. I'll have the nurse check you out in a little while, but you should be good to go home this morning. You'll have to take it easy for a few days. No aerobics or sports. If the headache comes back, check in with us right away, okay?"

"I will." She eased herself up on the pillow. "What time shall I tell someone to pick me up?"

"Oh, you should be out of here by nine or so." He scribbled something on her chart, put it back on the bottom of her bed and turned to leave. "I'll give you a prescription for pain, but go easy with it. Only use it when really necessary."

He was gone before she could thank him. She called Stephanie, forgetting how early it was until her cousin's sleepy voice told her they were still in bed.

The next two hours crawled by while she waited for the nurse to check her vital statistics. She played with the breakfast a smiling nurse brought her and abandoned it the moment Stephanie finally appeared.

By then she was dressed and pacing back and forth in front of the wheelchair that was supposed to carry her to the main doors.

"Well, you look perky, all things considered," Stephanie said, eyeing the wheelchair. "Are you going to ride in that thing?"

"No, I'm not." Clara looked down at her torn pants. "I look like a bag lady."

"You look like you've been in an accident." Stephanie threw a bag on the bed. "Here, I brought you some clean clothes."

"I'm going home in these." Clara shuddered. "I'm not spending another moment in this place. Let's go."

She led the way toward the door, surprised at how shaky her knees felt. It hurt to walk, and the lights bothered her eyes, but once she was outside in the fresh air, she began to feel better.

"The car's over here." Stephanie took her arm, and she was happy to lean on her as she made her way across the parking lot.

"I guess Dan called my mother last night," Clara said, as she eased herself onto the seat.

"Yes, he did. She was at the hospital last night. They wouldn't let us see you. They said you were sleeping." Stephanie started the engine. "You know what this means, don't you?"

"Yeah, I'll have to tell my mother all the gory details over and over again."

"No, I mean . . . the accident and everything."

Clara hesitated, unsure how much her cousin knew. "I'll have to get my brakes checked more often?"

Stephanie threw her an impatient glance. "Dan met us at the hospital last night. He told us someone cut your brake lines."

"Oh, great. Please tell me he didn't tell my mother."

"No, I don't think so. He left just as she got there."

"You're not to tell her, either. In fact, Dan didn't want me to tell anyone."

"I know. He told me." Stephanie paused, obviously unhappy. "You know we're in danger. I guess you're right. We should tell Dan everything we know."

"Which is practically nothing. Most of what we know Dan knows already. We know a lot of people had good reason to hate Ana, but that's common knowledge."

"We also know that Roberta Prince had a contract with Ana that gave her the store if something happened to Ana."

Clara sighed. "I guess we could tell him that, but he'd want to know how we knew."

"We'll tell him Frannie was gossiping."

Clara shifted to a more comfortable position. "The problem with that is that Frannie might know something that could put her in danger. Dragging her into this could only make it worse for her."

"So you're going to put yourself in jeopardy to protect Frannie?"

"Even if we told Dan what we know, there's no guarantee it will help him solve the case. So far, the killer hasn't tried to hurt Frannie, so he probably doesn't know she knows anything."

"That's if it is a he and not a she."

Clara gave her a sharp look. "You think Roberta killed Ana, don't you?"

"What do *you* think?"

"I don't know what to think." Clara passed a hand across her aching forehead. "I do feel strongly that Ana's killer was someone she knew. I just can't see someone dragging her kicking and screaming into the bookstore."

"Exactly what I think."

"I suppose Roberta could have done it, but we still don't know if she was even in town on Friday night."

"She was here on Saturday night." Stephanie pulled up outside Clara's house. "You told me that yourself."

Clara opened her eyes. "Well, I guess we'll have to find out where she was on Friday night. Though even if she was in town, I don't know what that would prove."

Stephanie looked annoyed. "All of this would have been a lot easier if you hadn't shut off the Quinn Sense. Without it, we're paddling around in circles going nowhere. Someone out there is trying to hurt you now, and we have no idea who it could be."

"I'm sorry. I'm doing my best." Clara felt ridiculously close to tears and climbed out of the car before she made an utter fool of herself. "I'll see you at noon," she muttered and started for the house.

"Hey, wait a minute!" Stephanie hung out the window. "You're not coming in to the store today!"

"Yes, I am." Clara held on to the fence to steady herself. "I'll go nuts if I have to stay in that house all day."

"But the doctor —"

"Said I had to take it easy, that's all. I'll be fine. I'll be there in a couple of hours." She turned her back and marched a little unsteadily up the drive to the front steps.

To her relief, she heard her cousin's car pull away from the curb. An hour or so of rest in her bedroom and she'd be fine, she told herself. Good thing her mother wasn't home to bug her.

After making sure all the doors and windows were locked, she took a shower, her heart thumping at every little sound. Lying on her bed, she tried to convince herself that no one was going to try to murder her in broad daylight. Still, she felt too uneasy to sleep.

Her head still ached, and she made a mental note to have the prescription the doctor gave her filled at the pharmacy next to Rick's hardware store.

Thinking of Rick brought back all her doubts about him. She couldn't get the memory out of her mind of the red pickup leaving the parking lot just a minute or two before she got to her car.

He was the first one to reach her after the crash. To make sure she was dead? Was that why he smashed the window? To finish the job before the medics got there?

She closed her eyes. It hurt to think. It hurt to believe that Rick might be a cold-blooded killer. Yet if she were to survive long enough to find out who killed Ana Jordan, she would have to stay on her toes. If that meant treating Rick as a possible suspect, then so be it. From now on, she couldn't trust anyone. And that was frightening.

12

Clara awoke to the jazzy sound of her cell phone and silently cursed as she reached for it. How stupid of her not to turn it off. Glancing at the clock, she caught her breath. She'd been asleep after all, for more than an hour. She'd have to hurry to make it to the store by noon.

Her mother's voice answered her tentative "Hello?"

"Oh, there you are. Thank the Lord. I called the hospital, and they said you'd left over two hours ago. Why didn't you call me?"

Clara slid out of bed, grabbing the bedside table as the room shifted around her. "I came home and fell asleep." She blinked, twice, and the room stopped spinning. "Sorry."

"I should think so. I was worried about you. Who brought you home?"

"Stephanie." She glanced at the clock

again. "I have to go, Mom. I'm supposed to be at the Raven's Nest in half an hour."

"How are you going to get there? I could come home and take you. They can do without me here for a little while."

"No, it's okay, Mom. I'll take the bus. I'll see about renting a car later, at least until I get the insurance on the other one."

It took her another five minutes to convince her mother she was well enough to go to work, and she had to scramble to shower and dress. She heard her mother's phone ringing as she was heading for the door.

She paused for a second, decided it was probably a survey or one of her mother's friends and left it ringing as she closed the door behind her.

At the bookstore, she found it full of customers, most of whom were in the Reading Nook enjoying coffee and scones. Stephanie greeted her with a look that clearly expressed her worry over her cousin's condition. She said nothing, however, though Molly rushed over and gave her a hug.

"Are you all right?" Molly peered up at her, her eyes full of concern. "Steph said your car was totaled. It must have been horrible when you realized your brakes weren't working."

Clara managed a brief smile. "It was. But I'm fine, except for a crashing headache." She glanced at her cousin. "I'm going over to the pharmacy to get this filled. Can you do without me until I get back?"

Stephanie nodded. "Take your time."

"Thanks." Clara stepped out into the street, blinking as the sunlight stabbed her eyes.

"I just heard the news. How are you?"

The voice seemed to come from nowhere, and she had to blink several times to focus before she recognized Frannie.

"I'm doing all right." She turned her back to the sun.

Frannie wore a pair of sunglasses that just about hid her whole face. "Roberta told me what happened," she said, her fingers twisting the strap of her shoulder bag. "How awful. You could have been killed."

"But I wasn't." Clara did her best to smile. "A night in the hospital and I'm as good as new."

"Well, I'm glad to hear it." Frannie looked down the street, and then back at her again. "Be careful, Clara. I wouldn't want anything to happen to you." She walked off, leaving Clara staring after her.

Was that a warning? *What is it Frannie knows? Damn it, Sense, where are you?*

Shaking her head, Clara headed for the pharmacy just as Roberta stormed out of the hardware store, her face dark with annoyance.

She looked at Clara as if she were something nasty she'd found in her sandwich and stalked across the road with complete disregard for the motorist who had to abruptly brake for her.

Clara would have given anything to go into the hardware store to find out what had upset Jordan's new owner, but no matter what excuse she came up with, Rick would probably catch on right away that she was simply being nosy.

When she came out of the pharmacy with the pills the doctor had prescribed, Rick was stacking rakes and shovels in the wooden barrel outside his store. After a mental battle with herself, she gave in to the impulse and walked up to him.

She spoke his name, and he spun around, brandishing the rake like a weapon. His expression changed when he saw her. "Clara! I thought for a moment you were the spider woman."

Clara raised her eyebrows. "Who?"

"That Prince woman." He jerked his head at Jordan's. "I call her the Black Widow. I swear she's capable of devouring a man whole."

He actually sounded sincere. Could it be that, after all, Roberta's comments about her relationship with him were nothing more than wishful thinking? If so, knowing how much Roberta wanted more, Clara could afford to feel sorry for her. "She can't be that bad."

"Well, she is." His brows drew together as he stared across the street. "I think she's after my store."

"I think it's more likely she's after your body."

The gleam in his eyes when he looked at her unsettled her. "Well, if she is, she's going about it all wrong."

She remembered what Roberta had said about marrying him. It seemed the lady was doomed to disappointment on that score. Her delight at the thought was so disturbing she cut off Rick's next words with a hasty, "Gotta go! See you later."

Not that Rick's relationship with Roberta was any of her business, of course.

Even so, her steps were considerably lighter as she hurried back to the bookstore.

"I saw you talking to Rick," Stephanie said, the minute Clara got inside the door. "Did you ask him for a date?"

"Why would she ask Rick for a date?" Molly asked, appearing from behind a bookshelf. She looked at Clara with great interest. "Do you like him?"

"No! Yes! No . . . Oh, for heaven's sake." Clara headed for the Nook, calling over her shoulder, "I'm going to take a pill."

"You should go home," Stephanie called out after her.

Ignoring her, Clara turned the corner and found the Nook empty of customers, except for Frannie, who sat in one of the armchairs. She had a book on her lap and was munching on a ham roll, with a can of soda on the table next to her.

She looked up when Clara came in and smiled at her. "Head still hurting?"

Clara nodded, then wished she hadn't, as once more pain sliced through her forehead. "I'm going to take something for it," she said, and reached for a paper cup next to the water cooler.

"Good idea." Frannie held up her book. "I've just finished reading Wayne Lester's book. It's wonderful. Would you like to read it?"

She held it out, and Clara took it from her. "It does look real interesting, but right now I've got so many books on my TBR list, it would be months before I could get

216

to this." She handed the book back to her and filled the cup with water.

"So, what pills did the doctor give you?" Frannie asked, a loud pop accompanying her words as she snapped open the soda.

Clara squinted at the label. "Vicodin. These things are pretty powerful, and they make you drowsy. I think I'll only take a half."

"Good idea." Frannie took a sip of her soda then added, "How are you getting to work without a car?"

"I took the bus this morning." Clara snapped a pill in half and dropped one half back into the bottle. "I'll see about renting a car later."

"I've got one you can use." Frannie wrapped up what was left of her roll and put it back into a paper bag. "I use my bike most of the time, and my car really needs to be out on the road. The battery runs down if it's sitting too long in the parking lot. Could clog the fuel system, too. You'd actually be doing me a favor by running it."

Surprised by the offer, Clara hesitated.

"It's not a fancy car," Frannie said, getting to her feet, "but it will get you back and forth until you can get another one."

Catching the defensive tone in her voice, Clara realized a refusal would probably offend the woman. "That's so very nice of you!" She thought about hugging her, then decided against it. Frannie was not the hugging type. "I'll take really good care of it."

Frannie smiled, her eyes lighting up as if she'd been given a surprise gift. "Great then." She walked over to the cooler and dropped her soda can into the trash bin. "I can go home and get it tonight and bring it back for you. Then you can give me a ride home."

Clara thanked her again, genuinely touched by the generous offer. It seemed there was a lot more to Frannie than she'd first thought.

She said as much to Stephanie after Frannie had gone back to Jordan's. "She such a timid little woman, but she's really good-hearted and pretty intelligent, too."

"She's had a tough life." Stephanie bagged a couple of books and handed the package across the counter to the waiting customer. "You know about her son, don't you?"

Clara shook her head. "I thought she wasn't married."

"She isn't anymore. She's been divorced for several years now."

"So what about her son?"

Clara never got her answer, as the two of them were too busy serving the customers

218

at the counter. Stephanie rang for Molly to join them, and Clara couldn't help noticing the change in the people waiting to be served the minute Molly stepped behind the counter.

More than a week after the murder and they still suspected her of killing Ana. Clara watched the young woman as she made the transactions at the register, seemingly unaffected by the frosty atmosphere surrounding her. Clara wasn't fooled for an instant.

Molly was hurting, and doing her best to hide it.

It reminded her that she hadn't yet taken Molly to task about her taking the day off and lying to Stephanie. As soon as things quieted down, she decided, she'd tackle the subject.

John Halloran ambled into the store around two and disappeared into the Nook, much to Clara's relief. She managed to avoid him when he returned to the counter with a book in hand, leaving Molly to wait on him.

Meanwhile, Stephanie kept glancing at the clock and finally told them, "I have to go and pick up my kids. Their friend's birthday party should be over by now." She looked at Molly. "If things are still busy at four o'clock, would you stay on for a while to help Clara? I don't think she should be here alone if it's busy."

"For heaven's sake." Clara smiled at her cousin. "Stop mothering me. I have enough of that from my real mother. I'll be just fine. It always eases up by late afternoon, anyway, and I'll sit in the Nook between customers."

Stephanie frowned, obviously reluctant to leave. "All right. But call me the second you feel you need help, all right?"

"I promise. Now *go*." Clara turned back to assist another customer, and after a moment or two of hovering, Stephanie left.

By three-thirty, the store was empty again, and Clara joined Molly in the Nook for a cup of coffee. Clara waited until they were both seated on the couch before casually saying, "John Halloran was in a couple of days ago. He said he saw you riding down the coast road on the back of your boyfriend's motorbike."

Molly's cheeks turned pink. "Er . . . yes. I wasn't feeling well, so he took me for a breath of fresh air. He thought it would help me feel better."

Clara studied her face. "And did it?"

"Oh, yeah. It's amazing how a ride along the coast road on a motorbike can blow the bugs out of your head."

"Really." *She's lying.*

Molly slid her gaze away and picked up her coffee. "We were busy today. That's good. How are you feeling, anyway?"

"I'm okay." Clara paused, then added, "I'm worried about you, though."

Molly shot her a nervous glance. "Me? Why me?"

"If you keep making up stories like this, you're going to end up in real trouble some day."

The pink in Molly's cheeks turned red. "I don't know what you mean."

"Yes, you do." Clara picked up her coffee. "You called in sick on Wednesday so you could go for a joyride with your boyfriend."

Eyes sparkling with resentment, Molly stood up. "So what if I did? Just about everybody does that at some time or other. It's not a crime!"

"No, it isn't." Clara put down her cup. "Look, Molly, all I'm saying is that when you get caught out in a lie it makes people wary of trusting you, and right now, can you really afford to do that?"

For a moment or two Molly looked as if she might explode; then, suddenly, all the fight went out of her, and she let out her breath on a sigh. "No, I guess not. Sorry."

"You don't have to apologize to me. You

let Stephanie down, though, and I suggest that next time you want a day off, just ask her. I'm sure she'll work something out for you."

"Okay. You're right." Molly looked at the clock and sat down again. "Seriously, though, how's the headache?"

Clara smiled. "It's still there. In fact, I think I'll take the other half of my pill." She patted her pants pocket and frowned. "I must have left them on the table." She got up and walked over to the cooler, letting out her breath in relief when she saw the bottle lying on the table.

She opened it and shook out the white tablets into her hand.

Just then the doorbell rang, announcing a customer.

"I'll go." Molly jumped to her feet and vanished around the corner.

Clara heard voices and realized there was more than one person out there with Molly. She couldn't see the half tablet, so she quickly broke another one in half and swallowed it down. Shoving the bottle into her pocket, she hurried out to help Molly.

Things slowed down considerably after the three customers left, and Clara insisted Molly leave at four, the end of her shift.

Time dragged after that, and she passed

the hours straightening up the magazine racks and restocking the shelves.

By six o'clock her head was hurting again, but she was reluctant to take another pill until she could go to bed and sleep it off.

If she was going to drive Frannie's car home, she didn't need to be any more drowsy than she was already. In fact, she couldn't wait to go home and crawl into bed.

Her knees and back ached, and there was something wrong with her wrist. It felt weak and hurt every time she tried to lift anything. Glancing at the clock, she wondered how long it would take Frannie to ride home and get the car.

What if she couldn't get it started? What if the battery had died from sitting too long in the parking lot?

She thought about calling for a cab, but then if Frannie came back for her she'd have a wasted journey, and without knowing Frannie's phone number, there was no way to get in touch with her.

She decided to wait outside for her. The fresh air would revive her somewhat, and she would be ready to go when Frannie got there.

After turning out the lights and locking up, she stepped out into the street. Clouds had blown in from the ocean, and she felt a sprinkle of rain on her face as she peered down the hill, hoping to see the lights of Frannie's car.

"Need a ride?"

He'd come up behind her, so quietly she had no idea he was there until he'd spoken.

She swung around, her heart bumping as she came face-to-face with John Halloran. She glanced across the street. Lights still blazed in the windows of Parson's Hardware. That meant Rick was still there. All she had to do was cross the street.

Before she could move, John laid a firm hand on her arm. "You don't look well. Let me help you down to my car, and I'll take you home."

"No!" Realizing she'd raised her voice, she made an effort to lower it. "Thank you, but I'm waiting for a ride."

John had dropped his hand the second she'd yelled at him. "Ah, yes. Well, then. I just thought . . ."

Out of the corner of her eye she saw the lights go out in the hardware store. "It's very kind of you," she said firmly, "but Frannie will be here any minute to pick me up."

John jerked his head in surprise. "Frannie? Oh, I thought —"

At that moment Rick stepped out into the

street. Catching sight of them, he waved, and she waved back, beckoning him to join them. He held up his hand in acknowledgment, then stooped to lock the door.

"Well, then, I'll be off," John Halloran said, and calling out good-night to Rick, he shuffled off down the hill.

Clara watched him go, wondering exactly what it was he'd thought. She didn't have time to dwell on it, however, as Rick was striding across the street toward her.

"How's the headache?" he called out before he reached her. "You took off so fast this afternoon, I didn't get a chance to ask you."

"Oh, it's okay. I'm taking pills for it." She fished the bottle out of her pocket to show him.

He took them from her and peered at them in the light from the streetlamp. "Vicodin! Good stuff. But be careful. They can make you fall asleep standing up if you take too many."

"I'm taking halves right now, so I should be okay."

"Good." He paused, then moved a little closer. "So, was there something you wanted?"

His face was in shadow now, and she couldn't quite tell his expression. "Ah . . ."

She had no idea why she'd signaled to him like that. Maybe she just didn't want to be alone on the street with creepy John. That would sound weird if she said that, though. Especially since he was apparently Rick's trusted employee.

"You forgot, right?" Rick bent his neck to look into her face. "That happens sometimes with concussion. Maybe you'd better get checked out at the hospital."

"No, no, it's okay."

"Well, in any case, I'll walk you to the bus stop. Or did you call a cab?"

"Neither. Frannie's on her way to pick me up."

"Frannie? I didn't know she had a car. She always rides a bike to work."

"I don't think she uses it much." She looked down the hill and saw the lights of a car coming up. Praying it was Frannie, she said lightly, "I was just going to ask you . . . ah . . . if you knew of a good place to rent a car."

"Ah." He seemed disappointed as he straightened. "Well, there's the rental agency at the bottom of the hill, but I've never rented a car so I don't know if —" He broke off as the approaching black sedan screeched to a halt across the street.

Frannie rolled down the window and

waved. "Sorry it took me so long. I had trouble getting it started."

Clara waved back. "I'd better go," she said, edging away. "Thanks, anyway."

Looking somewhat puzzled, Rick nodded. "Sure. Any time. Oh, wait! Here's your pills. You'll be needing them tonight."

She thanked him again and left him standing on the curb as she scrambled into Frannie's car.

All the way down the hill Frannie apologized for the condition of the car. "It's old, and it's been sitting around a lot," she said, as she deftly turned the corner at the bottom of the hill. "At least the brakes work."

She said it just as they passed the vacant lot, and Clara shivered.

"I'm sorry," Frannie said, sounding upset. "I shouldn't have said that. I wasn't thinking."

"No, it's fine." She tossed around for something to change the subject and seized on the only thing that came to mind. "Stephanie mentioned that you have a son. How old is he?"

It was a dark stretch of road, and she couldn't see Frannie's face, but she knew by the sudden tense silence that she'd mentioned a touchy subject. "I'm sorry," she said quickly, "I —"

"It's all right." Frannie's voice sounded surprisingly harsh. "Kevin is twenty-three. I don't see much of him now."

"He doesn't come and visit?"

"No one visits me anymore. Sometimes I feel as if I'm floating in a tiny boat all alone on an endless ocean."

Guessing that Frannie and her son were estranged, Clara was relieved when Frannie pulled up in front of an apartment complex.

"This is where I live," Frannie said, her voice still sounding weird. "You can keep the car as long as you like. I hope it runs okay. It's not all that reliable." She opened the door and scrambled out.

Worried now that she'd upset the woman, Clara slid over into the driver's seat. "Are you okay? I didn't mean —"

"I'm all right." Frannie raised her hand in farewell and hurried across the parking lot to the building.

Still feeling bad, Clara pulled out onto the street and headed for the corner. The sedan was a lot bigger than the compact she was used to, and it took her a few minutes to feel comfortable driving it.

The steering wasn't as positive. In fact, when she reached the corner, she had to give the wheel almost a full turn before the big car fully responded.

Thankfully, nothing was coming in the opposite direction, and she steered the car into the lane, vowing to remember the sluggish response.

Once home she called Stephanie, who answered with her usual out-of-breath "Hello?"

"I forgot to ask you today," Clara said, coming straight to the point, "what happened with Frannie and her son?"

"Can this wait?" Stephanie paused, then yelled, "Michael! How many times do I have to tell you — no basketball in the *house.*"

Clara heard the faint sound of a crash and a tinkling of glass, then her cousin's voice again, *"Michael!* I knew it. Wonderful. I gotta go. See you tomorrow." The line went dead, leaving Clara still without an answer.

She laid the phone down on the dresser, and as she did so, the weird shivery feeling she knew so well crept over her.

Find out. It's important. You need to know.

There was no doubt in her mind. The Quinn Sense was back, and she had better pay attention to it this time. For something told her that if she didn't, she could very well live to regret it.

13

"So, what are you going to do about a car?" Jessie asked, leaning her elbows on the dining-room table. "How did you get home tonight, anyway?"

Clara told her about Frannie's offer. "She was so nice about it," she added when she was finished. "She made it sound as if I was doing her a favor."

Jessie nodded. "Frannie's like that. Always anxious to please. I think she craves attention and goes out of her way to be nice to people so they'll like her."

"What happened to her son?" Clara laid her fork down on her plate and reached for her water glass. "She got real defensive when I mentioned him."

"Frannie's son is what they refer to now as mentally challenged."

Clara murmured her dismay. "How sad for her. She must have had a tough time raising him."

"She did. Her husband, Norman, took off when Kevin was five. I think he got tired of taking second place to the child all the time."

"That was terribly selfish of him."

"Yes, it was." Jessie absently fished a shrimp out of the salad left in the bowl and popped it in her mouth. "You know what was strange about that, though? When Kevin left high school, he went to live with his father. We never could understand why. Frannie wouldn't talk about it, and nobody really knows what happened. Though I did hear that he's working for his father in his construction business and doing really well."

Clara frowned. "Maybe Frannie was too strict or something, and her son felt he had more freedom with his dad."

"Maybe." Jessie yawned behind her hand. "Whatever happened, I don't think Frannie has seen much of Kevin since he left."

"That's what she said." Clara drained her glass of water. "It's so sad, though. Those years raising him alone must have been really hard for her. She must have sacrificed a lot for that kid, and that's the thanks she got for it. No wonder she seems so depressed all the time."

"Well, you know, if she'd kept up her appearance, she might have had a second chance at love. With all that long stringy hair and the shoddy clothes she wears, it's no wonder she can't get a man. You have to look hot if you want to snag a mate these days."

Clara squirmed on her chair. Jessie's words brought up the mental image of the pizza cook breathing down her mother's cleavage. It was a little too much to swallow. "Well, I think I'll do the dishes and go to bed." She pushed her chair back and stood.

"Leave the dishes." Jessie flapped purple fingernails at her. "I'll do them. You go to bed. You look like death warmed up. A good night's sleep will do you good. Take a couple of those Vicodin. I guarantee you won't wake up until the morning."

That was exactly what the doctor ordered, Clara thought, as she bent down to plant a kiss on her mother's cheek. Now, if she could just stop worrying about whoever it was who wanted her dead, she might just get that good night's sleep.

A few minutes later she shook a few pills from the bottle into her hand. Spotting a half pill, she picked it out and swallowed it down with a full glass of water.

She was about to climb into bed when she had second thoughts. Half a pill probably wasn't going to do the trick. Maybe she should take the other half that was still in the bottle.

Much as she despised taking medications, she hated the idea of a sleepless night even more. Reluctantly, she trudged back to the bathroom, where she'd left the bottle of pills.

Shaking them into her hand once more, she looked for the half pill. It wasn't in her palm, and she shook out the remaining pills. Still no sign of the half pill.

Frowning, she thought back over the day. She'd taken a half right after she'd got to the store, and broke another pill in half that afternoon. There should have been two halves in the bottle.

She turned the bottle upside down and shook it. Nothing fell out of it, and she stared at the pills still in her hand. Now that she was really looking at them, there didn't seem to be that many.

She looked at the label. The doctor had prescribed twenty-five pills. She counted the ones in her hand. Eighteen. Plus the one and a half she'd already taken and the missing half. There were five and a half pills missing.

Her mind reeling, she walked back to her bed and sat down on the edge of it. The pills had been in her pocket all the time, except for the hour or so she'd left them on the table in the Nook. Someone must have taken the pills out of the bottle.

Her heart began to thump as she tried to remember who had been in the Nook that afternoon. Lots of people. Most of whom she didn't know. As well as three people she did know. Molly, Frannie and John Halloran.

A sudden vision popped into her head, of Rick standing in the shadows, her bottle of pills in his hand.

No! It could have been anyone. Most likely someone alone in the Nook. Maybe Ana's killer? Waiting for an opportunity to drop the pills into her coffee, perhaps?

Now she felt scared. First thing tomorrow she'd talk to Dan. Though short of locking her up in jail, she couldn't see what he could do to help.

Maybe she should join forces with Frannie, since she seemed to be in danger, too. What about Stephanie? Could she be a target for the killer, as well? Then again, Stephanie had George to protect her.

She was feeling sleepy. Her mind felt fuzzy, and once more it hurt to think. Abruptly she got up from the bed, went back into the bathroom and swallowed another pill. Her head had barely touched the pillow before she was asleep.

She awoke the following morning with the same fuzzy feeling and staggered out of bed wishing fervently that she'd stuck with the half pill the night before.

It took three cups of strong black coffee to make her feel awake enough that she could safely drive the black monster parked in the driveway.

She left the house early, intending to stop by the police station on her way to the Raven's Nest. She drove carefully, aware of the big car's sloppy steering.

Arriving at the police station, she parked the car and walked across the parking lot to the front door. The offices were housed in what had once been a small theater. A golden arch adorned the redbrick front, upon which billboards had announced the shows. Inside the building, the sloping floor and ornate ceiling were all that was left of the original decor. The stage and seating had been torn out and partitioned off into cubicles.

A couple of small holding cells occupied what was once backstage, and a kitchen had been added onto the existing bathrooms.

Clara had been inside the police station only once before, on a grade-school tour.

It was long before she'd left for New York, and she still remembered hearing voices and smelling the overpowering odor of tobacco and perfume.

It wasn't until she'd mentioned it to Stephanie that she'd realized it was the Quinn Sense at work, and no one else had any inkling of what she could hear and smell.

Stepping inside the door now, she held her breath, waiting for the voices to disturb her again. Her shoulders sagged in relief when she could hear nothing but the ringing of a telephone and the tapping of computer keyboards. Even the smell had disappeared, leaving behind only the musty aroma of an old building.

She headed for Dan's office and knocked on the door. He called out to her, and she went in, taking the chair he offered her.

Frowning, he took off his reading glasses. "I wondered when you'd show up. You got my message, then?"

She stared at him, wondering what she'd missed. "What message?"

"I called your home yesterday and asked you to stop in."

"Oh." Now she remembered the phone ringing as she'd left the house the day before. "Mom must have taken the message and forgot to tell me." She sighed. "Though you'd think she'd remember something as important as a summons by the police."

Dan smiled. "Not exactly a summons. I kind of made it sound like a casual invitation. That's probably why your mom didn't take too much notice of it. I didn't want to send you all into a panic."

Clara nodded ruefully as she took the seat he offered her. "I do tend to panic lately. Guess that goes with the territory when someone is trying to kill me."

Dan's expression sobered at once. "No laughing matter, that's for sure. We're still investigating but haven't come up with anything concrete yet." He paused, then opened a drawer in his desk and took out a small plastic bag. "Can you tell me where you had your car parked the night of the wreck?"

Surprised, she answered a little sharply. "Where everyone parks their car. In the parking lot on Third and Main."

He gave her one of his tired-cop looks. "I meant exactly where in the parking lot?"

"Oh." Feeling foolish, she thought about it. "I was over by the bushes on the left side, opposite the exit."

"Ah. I thought so." He placed the bag on the desk in front of her. "We found some steel shavings in that area, along with this."

Clara picked up the bag and peered at the tiny, glittering object inside it. "What is it?"

"It looks like a whale to me."

She held the bag higher to the light from the window behind him. "Yes, it does. A tiny golden whale."

"The thing is, it's not so much what it is, but where it came from."

She felt a jolt and dropped the bag on the desk. "You think whoever tampered with my brakes dropped it?"

"Could be." Dan sat back on his chair. "I'm guessing it's one of those lucky charms. You know, like on a bracelet or maybe a key chain."

Clara caught her breath. "So all we have to do is find the bracelet or keychain —"

"Whoa, whoa, wait a minute." Dan picked up his glasses and perched them on his nose. "First off, we don't know that this belongs to the suspect. Even if it does, it'll be like hunting for a diamond in the sand. I just wanna know if you remember seeing anything like this on anyone in the past few days."

"Oh." Clara let out her breath on a sigh of disappointment.

She peered at the charm, fingering it

through the plastic. *You've seen this some-where.*

"I have?" she murmured. "Where?"

Dan sat up on his chair. "You have? You know who it belongs to?"

Clara jumped. She'd answered the voice out loud, forgetting where she was. "Oh, no, I mean . . . I think I've seen it some-where before, but I don't remember where. Maybe it will come to me later."

Dan's shoulders slumped. "Okay. It was a long shot, anyway. Just don't go beating yourself over the head trying to remember."

"If it belongs to whoever it was messing with my car," Clara said grimly, "I'm going to move heaven and earth to remember."

Dan looked alarmed. "Like I said, just because it was in the parking lot doesn't mean it belongs to our suspect. Anyone could have dropped it there, so don't go jumping to any wrong conclusions, okay?"

She nodded, her mind already working feverishly. Somewhere, sometime, she'd seen a bunch of gold charms. In a store window? If only she could remember. Maybe Stephanie would know.

Now she couldn't wait to get to the book-store. "I have to go. I'm late for work."

"Okay, but just be careful out there, okay?"

"I will." She jumped up and rushed for the door, leaving a startled police chief staring after her.

It wasn't until she walked into the Raven's Nest that she realized she'd forgotten to tell Dan about the missing pills.

Rick must have been right when he'd said a concussion makes someone forgetful.

It seemed as if everyone in town was in the store when she walked in.

"It's Sunday," Stephanie said, in answer to her cousin's raised eyebrows. "We're always busy on a Sunday."

Clara joined Molly behind the counter, while Stephanie disappeared in the direction of the Nook.

John Halloran was waiting to be served, and he seemed to be in a hurry as Molly swiped his card and handed him the books he'd bought. He practically snatched them from her and rushed for the door, colliding with a customer on his way out.

Clara was hoping to get a glimpse of John's key chain, but another customer kept her busy, and the last she saw of John, he was charging across the street toward the hardware store.

Clara hadn't recognized Tim Rozzi without his uniform until he nodded at her as he walked past the counter. "Feeling better?"

"Much better, thanks." She smiled at him, knowing it was a lie. She wasn't going to feel better until the killer was behind bars and she could feel safe again.

Rick came into the store soon after that, giving her a brief nod before heading down to the Nook. She barely had time to acknowledge him while trying to answer the questions of the teenager at the counter.

Molly nudged her as Rick vanished down an aisle. "There's your boyfriend."

"He's not my boyfriend, so don't start that rumor going around. Please."

Molly looked offended. "I didn't start it. Someone told me you two were engaged. I figured it was something you wanted kept secret, since Stephanie didn't say anything about it, but —"

Clara uttered a grunt of dismay. "Oh, no. I'd forgotten about that."

"About what? That you'd promised to marry the guy?" Molly shook her head. "How could you forget that? Though I have to say, you didn't waste any time. You've only known him a week, haven't you? Or did you meet him —"

"Oh, for heaven's sake!" Clara slammed a book on the counter, startling the young girl waiting to be served. "Who gets engaged after knowing someone one week? Of course we're not engaged. Rick told the ambulance driver that so he could ride to the hospital with me, that's all." She scowled in the direction of the Nook. "He promised me he'd clear all that up."

Molly grinned. "He conned a ride in the ambulance? Maybe there's more to the story than you're letting on."

Clara bared her teeth as she towered over Molly. "Not . . . one . . . more . . . word. Okay?"

Molly threw her hands in the air. "Okay, okay. I was just asking, that's all."

Clara frowned. "Who told you that, any-way?"

Molly raised her chin and stared thoughtfully at the ceiling. "Now, let me see . . ." She shook her head. "Sorry, can't remember. It could have been the mailman. I was talking to him this morning. Or maybe it was Sheila at the bank."

Clara groaned. First chance she got, she was going to have a word with Rick Sanders.

The customers kept coming, however, and Rick left the store without her having a moment to talk to him. In fact, she was so busy, it all went out of her head.

Things had just begun to slow down when

she answered her cell phone later that afternoon. To her dismay, she heard her mother crying on the phone.

"Why didn't you tell me?"

Clara deciphered the muffled words and silently cursed. Somehow her mother must have heard the news about her brakes being cut. "I didn't want to worry you, Mom. Besides, we don't know for sure. It could have been an accident."

"An accident?" Her mother's shocked voice seemed to echo in her ear. "Are you telling me you're *pregnant?*"

Clara blinked. "Pregnant? No, of course not."

Stephanie passed by at that moment and stopped short. "Who's pregnant? Not you? Why didn't you tell me?"

Clara tucked her phone against her chest and whispered fiercely, "I'm not pregnant!"

"You're pregnant?" Molly halted behind Stephanie, her eyes wide. "So that's why you're in such a hurry to get married."

Clara threw her head back and yelled, "For pity's sake! For the last time, I'm *not* pregnant!"

"You're getting married?" Stephanie took hold of her arm and shook it. "Why didn't you *tell* me? Who's the guy? Not the one in New York?"

Against her chest, Clara could hear her mother's voice wailing. Quickly she raised the phone to her ear.

"No one tells me *anything*," her mother sobbed. "My only daughter's getting married. Why am I always the last to know?"

"Mom." Clara briefly closed her eyes, then tried again. "*Mom!* I'm not getting married. I'm not pregnant. This is all a huge misunderstanding. The guy across the street told the ambulance driver that we were engaged because he didn't want me traveling to the hospital alone, that's all. He promised me he'd tell everyone what happened, but I guess he didn't get to it."

"What guy across the street?" Jessie asked, sniffing.

Clara sighed. "Rick Sanders, the owner of the hardware store."

"I know Rick." Jessie's voice brightened. "Are you two —"

"*No!* We're not anything, Mom. I have no interest in Rick Sanders whatsoever."

"Aw, and here I was planning the honeymoon." The familiar voice had spoken from behind her, and she spun around.

Rick stood at the end of the aisle, one hand resting on the bookshelf, the other covering his eyes in mock despair.

Stephanie and Molly melted away, while

Clara let out an explosive growl of frustration and charged over to the Nook. Relieved to find it unoccupied, she told her mother she was busy and snapped the phone shut.

To her immense dismay, Rick sauntered in behind her and headed for the coffeepot. "I was looking for a copy of this month's auto magazine. Stephanie couldn't find it this morning, and she said she'd look for it in the stockroom when she got time."

Keeping her back turned to him, Clara muttered, "She's been real busy. I'll take a look in there if you like."

"No rush. I can come back tomorrow."

She heard him pouring coffee into a mug and decided it was time to leave. "I'd better get back to the counter."

"Wait."

She turned to face him, her heart jumping when she saw his serious expression.

He put the mug down on the table, and folding his arms, he leaned back against the wall. "I'm sorry about the rumors. I really didn't think we were newsworthy enough to cause a sensation."

Clara felt her mouth twitch in spite of herself. "You underestimate your popularity. I imagine quite a few young women are heartbroken at the idea of losing Finn's Harbor's most eligible bachelor."

"Ouch." He winced. "Do I detect a note of sarcasm in those dulcet tones?"

She laughed. "Dulcet? Isn't that a little outdated?"

"Blame it on a fondness for Victorian novels." He unfolded his arms. "No, really, I'm sorry. I did go to the library to talk to your mom, but she was in a meeting, and I couldn't wait. I can come over to your house this evening and explain, if you like."

"Thanks, but it isn't necessary. I've already explained, and that should be enough."

She started to leave, pausing when he said quietly, "By the way, there are no heartbroken young women. At least, not on my account."

She smiled. "I was only joking."

"I know. I just wanted to set things straight."

She thought about it on her way back to the counter. Why wasn't he married? What was his story? Why did she even care? He could be a murderer for heaven's sake, though she still had a hard time believing that.

When she got back to the front of the store, Frannie was there talking to Molly, apparently not sharing the suspicions of the general public.

Only one other customer besides Rick

browsed the shelves, and Stephanie came up to join them at the counter. "I think I'm going home," she announced, glancing at the clock. "This has been a real busy day, I'm happy to say."

"Yes, it has." Molly reached for her purse. "It's time I left, too."

"I still have another four hours to go," Frannie said, turning to leave. "I'd better get back before Roberta comes looking for me." She paused at the door. "How's the car behaving, Clara?"

"It's great! You might want to get the steering checked, though. It feels a little unstable on the corners."

Frannie frowned. "It does? Oh, my. I'll certainly have to get that taken care of, right away. Perhaps you shouldn't drive it, Clara, if —"

"It's fine, really," Clara assured her. "I've gotten used to it now. I'll just take it a little slower on the bends, and I'll be fine."

Frannie still looked worried, shaking her head as she headed out the door.

Stephanie sighed. "That woman will get an ulcer one day. I don't know how she takes working for Roberta Prince. I thought Ana was bad enough, but Roberta is something else. Talk about a prima donna."

"Oh, look!" Molly jabbed a finger at the

counter. "Frannie left her book here. I'd take it in to her, but I'm late for a date." She ignored Stephanie's look of disapproval and ran out the door.

Stephanie shook her head. "I really worry about that girl. She'll end up in real trouble if she doesn't stay away from that hoodlum."

"Well, there's not a lot you can do about it. She's an adult, and she runs her own life." Clara picked up Frannie's book. "You go on home. I'll drop this off for Frannie before she leaves tonight."

Stephanie looked relieved. "Thanks. I know George will be waiting for me to get home. My mom's probably dropped the kids off by now, and he is most likely tearing his hair out."

Clara grinned. "George needs to toughen up."

"Tell me about it." Stephanie was out of the door before she'd finished speaking.

Clara went to clean up the Nook, then settled down on an armchair to read some magazines. The time passed quickly, with only one customer to interrupt her break. After the rush of the day, she was only too happy to put her feet up and enjoy a cup of coffee in peace.

With an eye on the clock, she checked out the cash register five minutes early, then picked up Frannie's book. After locking up, she hurried over to Jordan's, relieved to see the lights still on.

The store appeared to be empty when she went in, with no sign of anyone behind the long counter. She called out Frannie's name, hoping she hadn't missed her after all.

When no one answered her, she ventured farther into the store, still calling for Frannie. She was about to give up when the office door opened, and Roberta stepped out.

"Oh, sorry," she sang out when she saw Clara. "I didn't know anyone was here. I was about to lock up."

"I came in to see Frannie." Clara held up the book. "She left this on our counter this afternoon."

Roberta rolled her eyes. "That woman would lose her head if it wasn't attached to her shoulders. She left early today. Said she had something important to do."

"Oh." Clara looked down at the book in her hand. "Well, I could leave it here for her, or I could drop it off at her apartment."

"Oh, no, don't bother. She'll be in tomorrow morning. Here, give it to me."

Roberta held out her hand, and as she did so, Clara saw something glittering on her wrist.

She moved toward the other woman slowly, her gaze fixed on the shiny objects. As she got close, she held out the book, and Roberta stretched out her hand to take it. Dangling from her wrist was a gold chain, with several tiny gold charms.

Just like the one Dan had in the plastic bag in his office.

14

Clara froze, the book still held in her clenched fingers. Roberta dropped her hand, her face a mask of indifference. "Something wrong?"

Don't let her know what you know.

With an effort, Clara pulled herself together. "Oh, no. I was just admiring your bracelet, that's all. I've seen one like it in a store in New York. It's lovely."

"Oh, this?" Roberta shook her hand as if trying to rid herself of an offensive bug. "I don't know why I still wear it. It keeps catching on things. I've already lost three of the charms that way."

"Oh, what a shame." Clara fought to keep her voice steady.

"Ah, well, my own fault. I shouldn't wear it while I'm working. It was given to me by an old friend." She fingered the charms, her features softening. "It holds a lot of good memories for me. That's why I like to wear it. Reminds me of happier times."

Clara felt her throat drying up and coughed. "Well, I'd better get going. My mother will be wondering where I am."

"What about the book? Did you want to leave it here?"

Realizing she still held the book, Clara thrust it at her. "Tell Frannie I'm sorry I missed her."

"Of course." Roberta followed her to the door. "Sorry to hear about your accident, by the way. Frannie told me you're driving her car until you get a new one."

Clara's heart seemed to drop. "Ah . . . yes. I haven't had time to look for another one yet."

"I can't imagine anyone preferring to ride a bike all that way when she could drive. Then again, I guess it's a lot cheaper."

"I suppose so. Well, good-night!" Clara shoved open the door and practically fell through it.

She didn't look back until she was inside Frannie's car with the door locked. Letting out her breath, she tried to decide what to do.

Dan's words came back to her. *Anyone could have dropped it there, so don't go jumping to any wrong conclusions.*

Dan was right. After all, Roberta said

252

she'd lost three of the charms. She must park in the parking lot, too. She could easily have lost one of them just getting into her car.

She made her shoulders relax and turned on the engine.

Anyone who takes classes in auto repair just to meet men is not my idea of a good person. Clara's fingers clenched on the wheel. Frannie's words, talking about Roberta.

She had to talk to Dan again, and right now. She flipped open her cell phone and began to dial 911, then decided it wasn't really an emergency. Just a bunch of stuff that didn't necessarily add up. By now Dan was probably at home anyway. It would just have to wait until tomorrow.

She slept badly that night, waking up from a nightmare in the early hours of the morning. Bathed in sweat, she threw off the covers and padded to the bathroom for a glass of water.

She had no choice, she told herself, as she stared at her white face in the mirror. She had to tell Dan what she knew. Maybe it would be enough for Dan to at least take Roberta in for questioning. Then Frannie would be safe for a while and so would she. Having made up her mind, she went back to bed and another fitful sleep until the alarm woke her up.

Her mother was at the stove when she went into the kitchen.

The smell of bacon and coffee tempted her enough to sit down to the breakfast her mother had cooked, though it was hard to enjoy it with everything on her mind.

"Are you all right?" Jessie asked, passing her another slice of toast. "You look awful."

"I didn't sleep well." Clara took the toast and reached for the butter.

"Is it the bed? It's a new mattress but —"

"It's not the bed, Mom. The bed is fine. It's just . . . getting used to being here, that's all."

"You miss New York. I knew you would. I don't know why you came home to live. I knew you would be miserable."

"I'm not miserable." Deciding she didn't want the toast after all, Clara drained her coffee and pushed her chair back. "I'd better get going or I'll be late."

Jessie glanced at the clock. "You don't have to be there until noon."

"I have an errand to run first."

Jessie's forehead creased. "Is everything all right, Clara? You seem nervous, on edge. Is something worrying you? You're not hurting, are you? I mean, with the accident and everything?"

254

"No, Mom, I'm fine. Just tired, that's all." Clara dropped a kiss on her mother's cheek and fled.

When she arrived at the police station, Tim greeted her with a huge grin and a cheery "Hi there! What can I do for you?"

Clara nodded her head at Dan's office door. "I came to see the boss."

"Oh, he's not there. He had to go out of town for a couple of days. Is there something I can do?" Tim looked worried. "Someone giving you trouble again?"

Clara hesitated. She liked Tim, but she didn't feel the same sense of security she felt talking to Dan. "No, it's okay. I guess I'll wait for Dan to get back."

Tim's frown intensified. "You sure? If it's important, I'm sure we can take care of it for you."

"Thanks, but it's nothing, really. I'll come back in a couple of days." She left, trying to convince herself she was doing the right thing.

When Clara arrived at the store, Stephanie greeted her with an anxious frown. "You don't look good. Didn't you sleep well?"

Clara grunted. "Who can sleep well with all this stuff going on?"

"What stuff's going on?" Molly said from behind her.

Taken off guard, Clara floundered. "Ah . . . I was just . . . ah . . ."

"She's in love," Stephanie burst out, then cringed as Clara sent her a murderous look.

"With Rick?" Molly's eyes lit up. "How cool! Does he know?"

"Once and for all, I am not in love with Rick." Clara glared at her cousin again. "Nor anyone else, for that matter."

Molly shook her head. "I never know when you two are joking or not," she said, and marched off down the aisle to the stock-room.

Clara turned on Stephanie. "What the heck was that?"

Stephanie shrugged. "Sorry. I said the first thing that came into my head. Did you get things straightened out with Aunt Jessie, by the way?"

"Yes, I did. No thanks to you."

"Hey, I was just repeating what Molly was saying." She tilted her head to one side. "You know, it was awfully sweet of Rick to tell those guys you were engaged just so he could ride to the hospital with you. He's a really cute guy, you know."

Clara gritted her teeth. "Forget it, Miss Matchmaker. I'm just not interested."

Stephanie sighed. "Too bad. You could do a lot worse."

"He can't be all that amazing or he'd be married by now."

"He *was* married once. I don't know what happened, but he's been single for a few years now, so I heard."

Clara fought the temptation, then gave in. "Does he have kids?"

"Not as far as I know." Stephanie smiled as a customer approached the counter. "He hasn't mentioned them if he does. Why don't you ask him?"

"It's none of my business." The doorbell rang, putting an end to what was becoming for Clara an uncomfortable conversation.

She glanced at the door, surprised to see Frannie waving at her.

Hurrying over to her, she asked anxiously, "Is everything all right?"

Frannie nodded. "I just wanted to thank you for bringing over the book last night. I had completely forgotten about it until I got home, and then it was too late to come back for it. Roberta gave it to me this morning."

"Oh, you're welcome." Clara smiled in relief. "Have you got time for a cup of coffee?"

Frannie looked anxious. "I guess I could stay for a few minutes. Roberta's not in yet. She said she'd be late this morning."

At the mention of Roberta, Clara felt a cold tingle down her back. She led the way to the Nook, hoping they would be alone. Luckily, the last two customers were on the way out, and she had a few moments alone with Frannie.

After filling two mugs with coffee, she handed one to Frannie. "I wanted to ask you: the day of my accident, was Roberta at the store?"

Frannie stared at her for a long moment. "Why do you ask?"

"I . . . ah . . . thought I saw her on the hill that night, but I may have been mistaken."

"Oh." Frannie seemed to relax. "Yes, she was in the store that day. She came down for the weekend." She looked down at her mug. "I never thought I'd be working for her in just a few days. It's weird how things turn out, isn't it?"

"It sure is." Clara tried to suppress a yawn and failed. She took a sip of her coffee and murmured, "I really need this. I'm so sleepy today."

"Didn't you sleep well?"

"Nightmares. I woke up in the middle of the night. I had trouble getting to sleep again after that."

Frannie sank onto an armchair. "I hate when that happens. Funny thing, I had a nightmare the other night. I've been meaning to tell you. You were in it."

Clara sat down on the edge of the couch. "I was?"

Frannie shuddered. "Yes, it was awful. I saw you standing on a rock in the middle of a raging river, and there was a huge whale heading straight for you."

She cradled her coffee in both hands, as if trying to get warm. "I kept trying to shout at you to warn you that the whale was going to crash into you, but I couldn't get my voice above a whisper. It was getting closer and closer and nothing I could do could stop it, and . . ." She looked up, her eyes filled with anguish. "Then I woke up."

Clara's heart began to thump. Frannie's voice faded away, drowned out by other voices, all whispering, echoing each other in her mind. They were telling her something. Something desperately important.

She jumped up so fast she tipped her mug over, and coffee splashed down onto the beige rug.

"Oh, dear," Frannie said, gazing gloomily at the spreading brown stain. "That'll be hard to get out."

"Yes, it will." Clara bounded over to the sink and dragged two sheets of paper towel off the holder. Holding them under the faucet, she ran cold water until they were soaked.

"I've heard that egg yolk is good for coffee stains," Frannie said, leaning forward to watch her dab at the mess.

Clara gritted her teeth. "I don't happen to have any eggs handy right now."

"Ah, well, water and vinegar works, too."

"Or vinegar." *Please go. I need to think.*

"I could run next door and see if we have any in the store?"

Clara forced a smile. "Thank you, Frannie, but this seems to be working." She scrubbed harder, leaving tiny little pieces of paper towel embedded in the stain.

"Not very well," Frannie observed.

To Clara's utmost relief, Molly appeared at that moment.

"Wow! What happened?" She walked over to stare at the stain.

"Clara spilled her coffee," Frannie said helpfully.

"No kidding." Molly shook her head. "That's gonna be tough to get out."

"That's what I said." Frannie got up to take a closer look at the stain. "Egg yolks or vinegar. That's the answer."

Giving up, Clara wadded the last of the paper in her hand and stood up. "Guess I'd better go get some eggs and vinegar then."

She smiled at Frannie. "Thanks for the advice, Frannie."

Frannie's face lit up. "I'm happy to help. Any time." She glanced at her watch. "Oh, my, I'd better get back to the shop. Roberta will be back any minute. If she catches me in here, she'll cut my head off."

Clara clutched her stomach as Frannie dashed off, and Molly asked anxiously, "Are you okay? You look like you're going to hurl."

"I . . . I'm fine. Excuse me." Clara dashed for the restroom, the only place she was guaranteed to be alone. She sat in the end cubicle, holding her head in her hands, struggling to make sense of what the voices were telling her.

It was all too vague. Just when she thought she had grasped their meaning, other voices argued and contradicted, like a war of words in her mind.

She heard the restroom door open, and at the sound, the voices grew silent. For a moment, she felt only relief. Then the awesome responsibility of what she knew, or thought she knew, came crashing down on her.

"Clara? Are you all right?"

It was Stephanie's voice, strained with worry, and Clara stood up. "I'm fine," she called out, and flushed the toilet before leaving the cubicle.

Stephanie's face was creased with concern. "Molly said you looked as if you were going to throw up."

"Guess it's the aftereffects of the concussion. I feel better now, so quit worrying."

Stephanie narrowed her eyes. "Has something happened?"

Clara sighed. She never had been able to get anything past her cousin. "Maybe. We need to talk, but not here. I'll come over to your house this evening, if we can find somewhere private to talk."

"Of course. Come to dinner."

"Sounds good. By the way, I spilled coffee on the rug."

"I know. Molly told me. Don't worry, I'll get it out with vinegar."

Clara followed her cousin out into the store, making a mental note to keep vinegar on hand in the Nook in future.

There were enough customers to keep her mind busy for the rest of the day. When it came time to lock up, however, all her misgivings came rushing back.

Luckily her mother had plans for that evening, so Clara could at least escape an awkward conversation about why she was invited to dinner at Stephanie's when Jessie was not.

Sharing a meal with the Dowds usually meant dealing with childish arguments, robust voices and a lot of laughter in between.

That evening was no exception, as Olivia and Ethan fought over whose turn it was to pick up after the dog, Michael insisted on singing painfully out of tune a song he'd learned at school and George somehow managed to pour gravy over the edge of his plate onto the white tablecloth.

"You're worse than the kids," Stephanie told him, while her offspring giggled. "Now you can clean it up."

"Vinegar," Clara said, mopping up the gravy with her napkin. "Works wonders, or so I heard."

Stephanie rolled her eyes. "You heard that from me."

"And from Frannie." Clara paused, remembering why she was there.

Stephanie must have sensed her change of mood, as she put down her fork. "Clara and I have some things to talk over," she announced, "so we're going to my sewing room, and I don't want to be disturbed by anyone for *anything*. Got that?"

All three kids nodded.

"What about the dishes?" George asked.

Stephanie sent him a sweet smile. "I

thought you would do that for us, honey. Get the kids to help."

Her words were greeted with groans and moans. George's were the loudest of all.

Getting to her feet, Stephanie jerked her head at Clara. "Let's go, before these poor souls break my heart."

Clara followed her down the hallway to what once was a walk-in closet and now served as her cousin's sewing room. The narrow room was confining yet cheerfully decorated with collages that used to be Stephanie's passion and hobby before she bought the bookstore.

"So tell me," Stephanie demanded, "what's going on? What have you found out?"

Clara would have smiled if she hadn't felt so tense. "I don't know that I've found out anything. That's the problem."

Stephanie sat down on a fold-up chair in front of her sewing machine. "What does that mean?"

Clara dragged a bean bag chair around to face her cousin and plopped onto it. "You know how I used to be able to interpret dreams?"

"Of course. We were just talking about it the other day."

"Well, I think I've interpreted someone's

dream, and it told me who killed Ana."

"No way! Who is it?"

"I can't tell you right now. I'm not sure if it was the Quinn Sense or if it was my own instincts kicking in again. I don't want to say anything in case I'm wrong and another innocent person gets blamed for Ana's murder."

"Well, you can tell me, can't you?"

"I'd rather not."

Stephanie puffed out her breath. "Well, all right, be like that. What if I tell you I've come up with a plan to catch the murderer?"

Clara stared at her. "What kind of plan?"

"It's simple, but effective." Stephanie leaned forward, her face flushed with excitement. "You tell your suspect that we've found evidence that will incriminate the killer. That we've hidden it in a chocolate box on a shelf in the stockroom until Dan gets back. The killer will want to get to that evidence before the police get their hands on it. We'll be waiting in the stockroom to catch the killer red-handed." She sat back, beaming. "Clever, don't you think?"

Clara gulped. "I think it's insane. Not to mention dangerous."

"Not with two of us there. I'll take a picture with my cell phone while you call 911, and then we get out. I've got an empty chocolate box downstairs. It's the perfect plan, really."

"What if we have to wait up all night?"

Stephanie shrugged. "I can stay awake. What about you?"

"I mean what about George? Isn't he going to wonder where you are? What you're doing out all night?"

Stephanie's face fell. "Crap." She brightened. "I'll tell him we're taking inventory. I'll say it will take most of the night because we can't do it while the store is open."

"And he'll believe that?"

"Of course." Stephanie grinned. "He's very trusting, my George."

Clara shook her head. "This is crazy. If we're going to do something this dangerous, we should at least wait until Dan gets back."

"May I remind you that the killer is trying to kill you, too? You could be dead by the time Dan gets back."

"Thank you. That's very comforting."

Stephanie punched her cousin's shoulder. "Come on, it will be like old times."

"Not quite." Clara rubbed her arm. "Remember when I said that if things looked dangerous we'd talk to Dan?"

"Dan's not here."

"We could talk to Tim."

"And tell him what? You said yourself, you're not sure if you're right about this. That you don't want another innocent person blamed for Ana's murder. This way we can prove who the killer is and there'll be no doubt. Tim can make the arrest and it will all be over by the time Dan gets back."

Wavering, Clara murmured, "It does sound simple."

"I told you it was."

"But then your plans always do seem simple until we try to carry them out. Remember when we rounded up all the dogs in the neighborhood and took them to the park to play? We had a lot of really angry neighbors out all night looking for their pets, remember? That was a really good plan."

Stephanie pouted. "We were *five* for pity's sake. How were we to know the dogs wouldn't do what they were told." She started to grin. "It was fun, though."

"Well, we're not dealing with angry neighbors or runaway dogs now. We're dealing with a dangerous and unpredictable killer. We could both get badly hurt, or worse."

"So, what do you want to do? Wait for Dan to come back, and tell him you think you know who killed Ana because of someone's dream?"

Clara buried her face in her hands. "All right. We'll do it your way. But I don't have to like it."

"So now tell me who you think killed Ana Jordan."

"No, it's safer that you don't know. When are we going to do this anyway?"

"Tomorrow night. Molly will be leaving at two, so we won't have to worry about her finding out what we're doing." She paused. "It's not Molly, is it?"

"No," Clara said quietly. "It's not Molly. At least, I don't think so, and that's all I'm saying. Now I have to go home and come up with an excuse why I won't be home tomorrow night." She opened the door, then paused. "What if my suspect comes into the shop while we're open and gets into the stockroom?"

"You don't tell the suspect about the evidence until ten minutes before we close. I'll be in the stockroom already, waiting. You'll have to leave by the front door, lock up, then sneak around the block and come in the back door."

"Something tells me we're both going to regret this."

Stephanie narrowed her eyes. "Is it the Quinn Sense telling you?"

Clara smiled. "No. Just my own instincts

this time."

"Good. Then let's do it. Here we go, the Quinn cousins on the trail of adventure again!"

It was all very well for Stephanie to make light of it, but Clara was filled with misgivings. So many things could go wrong.

Yet she, more than anyone, wanted the killer caught. She was tired of looking over her shoulder, wondering where the next attack would come from. Stephanie's plan might just work, and on the surface, at least, it seemed no less dangerous than allowing whoever killed Ana the opportunity to kill again.

Sending up a silent prayer, she led the way back to the kitchen.

15

Rick came into the store the following afternoon. He said he was looking for a new cookbook but spent most of the time browsing through the magazine rack. He was still there when John Halloran walked into the store, wearing a smirk that instantly rattled Clara.

"I thought I'd find you in here," he said, walking up to Rick. "There's a young lady across the street, asking for you. I told her I'd try to find you. She seemed pretty anxious to talk to you."

Rick scowled. "Who is she?"

John shrugged. "She didn't give me her name."

Rick glanced at Clara, who immediately dropped her gaze.

Cursing herself for always getting caught staring at him, she ducked below the counter and pretended to be busy sorting out the catalogs.

"All right, tell her I'll be right there," Rick said, and a short moment later, the doorbell jingled.

Thinking they had both left, Clara shot to her feet and came face-to-face with Rick.

He stood on the other side of the counter, holding out a couple of magazines and wearing a silly grin. "I'll take these," he said, fishing out his wallet from his back pocket.

Wondering why the man always made her feel nervous, she took the bills he handed her and tried not to think about Stephanie's words. *You do get all twittery when you're around him.* It occurred to her that if Stephanie realized that, so might Rick, and the idea made her hand shake as she punched out the purchase on the cash register.

She handed him the change, trying not to flinch at the contact of her fingers on his palm. "Thank you, sir. I hope you enjoy them."

"Oh, I know I will." He lifted his hand in a mock salute and left her staring after him.

She watched him cross the street, and just as he reached the door of his store, a young woman flew out and wrapped her arms around his neck. They were still hugging when they disappeared inside.

Clara ignored the stab of disappointment. What else could she expect? Rick was a healthy, good-looking young man, and it would have been naive to think he had no girlfriends. Then again, it was only two days ago that he'd more or less told her there were no women in his life.

Which just goes to prove her theory, she told herself. No man can be trusted to tell the truth, the whole truth and nothing but the truth.

Her bad mood lasted the rest of the afternoon and into the evening. She had a hard time hiding it when Stephanie arrived, out of breath as always and talking nonstop.

When Clara wasn't as responsive as Stephanie would like, she turned on her, demanding, "What's the *matter* with you? I thought you would be excited about catching Ana's killer. You're not chickening out on me, are you?"

"Of course not." Happy to blame her cranky response on their imminent venture, she added, "Guess I'd better go tackle phase one of your plan."

Stephanie's eyes narrowed. "You're going next door to Jordan's, aren't you?"

"Maybe." Clara headed for the door. "You'd better get in the stockroom before someone sees you. I'll be back in a few minutes."

The sun hadn't quite set when she stepped

outside. Long shadows stretched along the sidewalk, and lights were popping up in windows all the way up the hill. Clara glanced at Parson's Hardware out of the corner of her eye. The lights were still on, so Rick hadn't closed up shop yet.

She wondered if the girlfriend was still there, then reminded herself it was none of her business. Determined not to waste time speculating on stuff that didn't concern her, she turned her back on the store and paused in front of Jordan's Stationer's.

Every instinct urged her to walk away. It was a crazy plan and probably wouldn't work anyway, and they'd be up all night for nothing. On the other hand, if it did work, they would be confronted by someone who had killed before and probably wouldn't hesitate to kill again.

She couldn't let her cousin expose herself to that kind of danger. Stephanie had kids to consider. If anything happened to their mother, what would they do? How would George manage?"

She half turned, but just then the door of Jordan's opened and a customer walked out. Seeing Clara standing there, he paused to hold the door open for her.

Clara hesitated, then thanked him and walked into the store.

■ ■ ■ ■

Alone in the Raven's Nest, Stephanie wandered down the aisle to the stockroom, pausing to examine the shelves every now and then. The longer she put off actually going into the stockroom, the more nervous she felt about it.

The plan had seemed so simple when she'd first blurted it out to Clara. True, she hadn't thought it through, but she'd seen it done on TV more than once, and it always worked. So why shouldn't it work now?

She went over the whole scenario in her head, as she had done a hundred times since Clara had left the night before. All they had to do was choose a place to hide close to the back door, so they could scoot out the minute she took a photo.

The killer would be taken by surprise and blinded by the flash, which would give them plenty of time to get out and call 911. Then run like hell until they got to the parking lot.

Stephanie had considered parking her car across the street, but since parking there was illegal, it would be just her luck for Tim to come along and make her move it. Besides, it might tip off the killer.

No, it had to be this way. She only hoped she could still run as fast as she used to when she and Clara played softball. She caught her breath. That was sixteen years ago. Hard to believe. A few pounds had found their way to her hips since then. She hoped they wouldn't slow her down.

Now that she was really thinking about it, the whole plan seemed a bit risky. Still, it was too late to change things now. Clara was probably next door, already halfway through her story, and the trap was about to be set.

Squaring her shoulders, Stephanie opened the stockroom door and flicked on the light. Studying the boxes piled up in the corner, she assured herself the little fort looked natural.

She'd decided that afternoon that the best place to hide was in the corner, by the back door. She'd moved some boxes around, piled them up a bit higher and created a perfect hiding place.

Now, all she had to do was wait for Clara to come back, and that should be any minute now. Standing behind the wall she'd built, she wondered how she would see the killer in the dark well enough to take a picture. Then again, the killer would surely have a flashlight in order to find the chocolate box, which she'd placed on a shelf clear across the room.

She should have thought to bring one. They might need one to find their way out in a hurry. Annoyed with herself for not thinking of it before, she hurried over to the door. She'd put a flashlight in a drawer under the counter the day she'd opened the store. It should still be there.

She flicked off the light and was halfway up the aisle when the shrill ringing of the phone startled her. A quick glance at the clock told her it was almost closing time. It had to be Clara. Something must have happened.

She rushed over to the counter and snatched up the receiver.

It wasn't Clara's voice that answered her, however. It was the voice of her husband, and he sounded unusually agitated.

"Steph? I'm sorry, honey. I'm at the hospital."

"Hospital?" She felt sick. "What happened? Are you hurt?"

"It's not me." His pause filled her with dread. "It's Olivia. She's had a really bad accident."

Stephanie let out a cry of anguish. "Oh, George! I'll be right there." He went on talking, but she didn't wait to listen. All she could think about was getting to her daughter's side as quickly as possible.

Snatching up her purse, she flew out the door, not even bothering to lock it behind her.

Clara walked cautiously up to the counter, where Roberta stood sorting through some papers. Frannie hovered nearby and sent her a smile, while Roberta looked up with her usual stiff-upper-lip expression.

Clara had rehearsed her speech, but a lot depended on the responses she got. Ad-libbing was not one of her strongest points, so she could only hope and pray that the conversation went the way she wanted it to go. "I noticed the other day that you had some calendars for next year," she told Roberta. "Do you have any with pictures of New York? I want to find one for my mother."

Roberta looked as if she couldn't care less. "I'm not sure. Frannie will take a look for you."

"Oh, that's okay." Clara smiled at Frannie. "I can look for myself. I just thought you might save me hunting through them, that's all."

"The calendars are over there," Frannie called out, pointing across the room.

"Thanks." Clara turned back to Roberta. "So, I've been meaning to ask you. How are things going? Do you need any help with anything? It must be so hard, having to take over from Ana after the way she died."

"It hasn't been easy, but we've managed, thanks." Roberta went back to shuffling her papers.

"It makes me sick to think of the killer still roaming free out there. Kind of creepy." Clara's shudder was just a little exaggerated.

"I should think he's probably long gone by now," Roberta muttered.

"Oh, do you think so? Well, I hope he hasn't gone too far." Clara looked around, then leaned across the counter and just slightly lowered her voice. "In any case, he won't be free for much longer."

Roberta gave her a suspicious look. "What do you mean?"

"I mean, he's going to be arrested any day now." She looked around again at the empty store, as if making sure no one else could hear her. "Stephanie and I just found evidence that will put him behind bars for the rest of his life."

She had Roberta's full attention now. The woman's eyes seemed to glaze over, and she ran the tip of her tongue over her lips before asking, in a voice thick with tension, "What kind of evidence?"

"Well, I can't really say." Clara leaned closer. "We've hidden it in a chocolate box." She briefly closed her eyes, aware of how silly all this must sound. Why would anyone believe such nonsense? It was too late to back out now. All she could do was hope she sounded convincing. "Stephanie put it on a shelf in the stockroom for safety," she went on, "just until Dan gets back to town. Then we'll give it to him, and you can bet he won't waste any time going after the killer."

From farther down the counter, Frannie uttered a quiet whimper.

Roberta seemed not to hear her. Her gaze was locked on Clara's face as she crumpled the papers in her hand. "Do you know who killed Ana?"

Clara shook her head and started backing up to the door. "No, not me. I don't want to know. Let the police do their job, that's what I say. I'm going home and plan to forget all about it until tomorrow, when Dan gets back."

"What about the calendar?" Frannie called out.

"I'll come in tomorrow. I'll have more time to look then. I have to go back now and lock up." With a quick wave of her hand, Clara was through the door and hurrying back to the bookstore.

Once inside, she looked around for Stephanie. Finding no sign of her, she figured her cousin was waiting for her in the stockroom. At least so far the plan seemed to be going along okay.

Now all they had to do was wait for the killer to show up. That was the part that Clara was nervous about. Still, she'd come this far, she might as well go through with the whole thing now.

Quickly she checked out the cash register, locked everything up securely, then made herself walk casually to the front door and step outside.

The keys rattled in her hand, and she had trouble fitting one of them into the lock, but finally she got it all locked up. The wind was stronger now, blowing her hair into her eyes as she zipped up her jacket and headed down the hill.

When she reached the corner of the block, she threw a quick glance over her shoulder to make sure no one had followed her, then darted around the corner and fled down the street to the wide alley that ran behind the stores.

Grabbing the handle of the back door to

the Raven's Nest, she gave it a sharp turn, but it refused to budge. Frowning, she rattled it. Stephanie must have forgotten to unlock it.

She rattled it again, waiting impatiently for her cousin to open the door. *Where was Stephanie?* She had to be in the bathroom or something. Again she rattled the handle. Still no response.

Something was wrong. The Sense was so strong, she could actually feel Stephanie's fear. Surely the killer couldn't have gone into the store and found her cousin while she was racing around the block?

Panic swept over her, and for an instant her mind blanked everything out. *Stephanie's in trouble. Get back inside the store.*

Clara twisted around and ran back around the block to the front door. Feverishly she unlocked it, glancing over her shoulder at the windows of Jordan's Stationer's. As she looked, the lights went out.

Without turning on the lights in the bookstore, Clara slipped inside and quickly closed the door, locking it from the inside.

"Stephanie?" She hissed the name in a loud whisper. "Are you in here?"

Her heart thumping, she listened for an answer. *Nothing.*

A faint glow from the streetlamps outside

threw dark shadows down the aisles. She could barely see to the end of them, and she crept along each one, fearing to see the limp body of her cousin lying somewhere on the floor.

Having satisfied herself that Stephanie was nowhere in the store, Clara moved slowly toward the stockroom. Stephanie had to be in there. If she was, there had to be a reason why she hadn't opened the back door.

Clara swallowed hard. She wouldn't think about the possible reasons. Stephanie had to be in that stockroom, alive and waiting for her. She just had to be.

The door handle twisted silently in her hand, and she eased the door open. As she did so, the beam of a flashlight swept across the floor.

Annoyed with her cousin for frightening her, Clara grunted and flipped on the stockroom light. "Stephanie! You scared me! Why on earth didn't . . . you . . ." Her voice faded into silence.

Standing before her, flashlight in one hand, the chocolate box in the other, was Frannie.

Stephanie's first thought when she saw her youngest son's stricken face and Olivia lying in the hospital bed was that her daughter was dying. None of George's assurances would convince her, and it wasn't until Olivia sat up and asked for ice cream that she dared to think that the child would recover.

"It's just a broken arm," the doctor said, showing her the X-ray. "A clean break. A few weeks and she'll forget it ever happened."

"*I* won't forget," Stephanie said, glaring at George. "In fact, I'd like to know exactly how it happened."

George looked uneasy. "Olivia was roughhousing with Michael and wouldn't quit when I told her to, so I sent them both to their rooms."

Olivia started to say something, but Stephanie hushed her with a sharp lift of her hand. "So then what happened?"

George looked up at the ceiling. "She wanted to go see you at the store. I told her she couldn't."

"Mom, I —" Olivia began, and again was shushed by her mother's threatening hand.

"And . . . ?"

"She fell out the window," Michael said.

"I didn't *fall* out of the window," Olivia said scornfully. "I climbed out. It was the tree I fell out of."

Stephanie clutched her stomach. "Oh, my

God. You are *never* to do that again, you hear me?"

Olivia nodded. "I won't," she promised. "It hurts when you fall out of a tree."

"I meant you are never to climb out of your *window* again." Stephanie shook her head. The memory of her and Clara climbing out of a bedroom window was all too clear in her head.

Clara. "Oh, *crap!*" She'd said it so loud two nurses frowned at her as they walked by.

"What now?" George said, alarm ringing in his voice.

Stephanie didn't answer. She was too busy scrabbling for her cell phone.

16

Time seemed to freeze as Clara stared at Frannie's frightened face. There were so many things she wanted to say, but none of them presented themselves in words. All she could do was stand there, waiting for Frannie to say something — anything — that would break the tension holding them fast.

Finally Frannie lifted the box in her hand and shook it. "It's empty."

It was such an anticlimax Clara felt an insane urge to laugh. "Frannie, what are you doing here?"

Frannie sent a hunted look around the room, as if seeking a way to escape. "Roberta sent me over here to get the box. I guess she wanted to know what was inside it."

Clara felt the tension easing in her shoulders. "We both know that's a lie, Frannie. In fact, you've been lying all along."

Frannie shook her head. "No, I —"

Clara stepped forward. "You were in the stockroom the night Ana died. Molly didn't tell you about Wayne Lester's book. She couldn't have. She left the bookstore a good half hour before you left Jordan's that night. You saw the boxes of that book the night you killed Ana Jordan."

For a long moment Frannie's features were set in a stubborn frown, then in an instant her face was transformed. She seemed to crumple up and shrink, like Alice in Wonderland.

She dropped the box, her knees gave way and she sank to the floor, tears running down her face. "I didn't mean to kill her," she said, and started crying in a hopeless way that tore at Clara's heart.

Okay, so Frannie had struck down a human being and taken a life. But right then, the woman seemed so utterly defenseless and alone, and Clara knew exactly how that felt.

She rushed forward and dropped to the floor by Frannie's side. With one arm around her, she murmured, "I know you didn't mean to, Frannie."

"I d-didn't mean to hurt you, either." Frannie gulped, struggling to control her sobs. "I j-just wanted to frighten you, so you wouldn't keep on looking for Ana's killer."

"You dropped Roberta's charm by my car to make it look as if she had messed with my brakes."

"I just wanted to confuse everybody, that's all."

"And you took Vicodin pills out of my bottle?"

"I wanted to scare you into giving up."

"You know everyone thought Molly had killed Ana," Clara said, with more than a hint of reproach.

Frannie nodded. "I'm sorry. I was hoping they'd all forget about it soon." Her entire body shuddered. "I know I've done some dreadful things. I don't know what came over me. It was as if all the lousy stuff Ana said and did over the years just all got bottled up until that night." She flicked a glance at Clara through wet lashes. "Did you know that she was going to burn down the Raven's Nest?"

Shock stole whatever words Clara had in her mind. She shook her head, grappling with the enormity of what it would have meant to Stephanie had Ana succeeded.

"She hated Stephanie, you know," Frannie went on. "She was always telling me how Stephanie stole George away from her in high school and it ruined her life. She never married. I don't think she ever got over losing George."

Clara finally found her voice. "So what happened that night?"

Frannie was silent for a long time, obviously reliving it all. When she finally spoke, her voice was low and calm, as if reciting a poem. "It was all about my son, Kevin. He had . . . problems when he was growing up. He was a slow learner. Kids made fun of him. His dad left us, and it was hard, raising him on my own. When he finally graduated, I asked Ana if she would hire him. She refused." Frannie drew a trembling breath. "She said she didn't want *that freak* working in her store. I never liked her after that."

Clara clenched her teeth. "I'm not surprised."

"Kevin thought I was the one stopping him from working there. I couldn't tell him what Ana had said. He was convinced I was ashamed of him and didn't want him working in town. He never forgave me."

"I'm so sorry."

Frannie appeared not to hear her. She seemed lost in her story, as if she were talking to herself. "Norman, my ex, was in Philadelphia, doing well in the construction business. He offered Kevin a job. So he went to live with his dad. I lost my son because Ana wouldn't give him a job. I *hated* her."

Clara jumped at the sudden venom in Frannie's voice. "Why did you go on working for her?"

Frannie shook her head. "I don't know. I'd worked there for so long, I guess I was afraid to look for another job. Or maybe I wasn't going to let her force me out. Whatever it was, that night, it all came to a boil."

She shivered, wrapping her arms across her chest. "Ana still had a key to this back door, from when it used to be part of Jordan's. She told me she was going to get rid of the bookstore once and for all. She made me go with her, to keep watch and make sure no one saw her light the fire."

Frannie looked up, tears spurting from her eyes again. "I couldn't let her do that to Stephanie. Your cousin has always been so nice to me. She didn't deserve to lose her store. We got in here, and I told Ana that if she set fire to the stockroom she'd burn down Jordan's as well. She said she didn't care. It wasn't hers anymore. She'd sold the business to Roberta."

Clara remembered what John Halloran had told her. Ana had been looking at property in Portland. Roberta had bought the business before Ana died. "So you knew Roberta was the legitimate owner?"

Frannie sniffed and wiped her nose with the back of her hand. "I didn't tell you because I thought the more suspicious other people looked, the less likely it was that anyone would find out it was me. That's why I said that I thought Roberta might have killed Ana to get the store."

Clara puffed out her breath. Obviously the Quinn Sense still wasn't reliable. In the old days she would have known at some point that Frannie was lying well before she interpreted her dream. "So then what happened?"

Frannie started rocking her thin body back and forth. "I told Ana that if she set fire to this place I'd tell the cops what she'd done. She said she'd tell them I did it. She said the cops would believe her because everyone knew I was retarded. *Just like my son.* That's when I lost it. I saw the bust, I picked it up," she raised her hands above her head, "and I *smashed* it as hard as I could on her head." She swung her hands down, making Clara shudder.

Sick to her stomach, she dropped her arm and sidled away from Frannie. It was so hard to believe that this quiet, inoffensive little woman had taken the life of someone and tried so hard to put the blame on someone else.

"I didn't mean to kill her. I just wanted to shut her up," Frannie said, beginning to cry again. "I knew she was dead and I didn't know what to do. I thought about calling the cops, but then I got scared at what they might do to me. I got out of there and went home, and started thinking how I could confuse everyone so they wouldn't find out it was me. I'm so s-sorry . . ."

Clara struggled for the right words to say, but before she could speak, a deep voice spoke from the doorway, startling them both.

"I guess that's all I need."

Clara scrambled to her feet as Tim walked into the room, one hand resting on his holster. "Frances Dearly, you are under arrest for the murder of Ana Jordan. You have the right to remain silent. Anything you say . . ."

The rest of his words went over Clara's head, for at that moment Rick appeared in the doorway behind the officer, his face a mask of apprehension.

He caught sight of her and strode over to her, grasping her upper arms to peer into her face. "Are you all right?"

"I'm fine." She looked from him to Tim

and back again. "How did you —"

"I saw you go back into the store without putting the lights on. Then I saw Tim get out of his car and walk down the alley. I figured something was wrong and followed him." He let go of her and glanced at Frannie, who was quietly crying as Tim put handcuffs on her. "She killed Ana?"

"Yes, but Tim —"

Tim held up his hand. "I'm taking her down to the station. You're okay to lock up here?"

"Of course, but Tim —"

He gave her a quick shake of his head. "Not now."

Clara watched him lead the sobbing woman out the door. She felt like crying herself.

"How did all that happen?" Rick asked, bending down to pick up Frannie's flashlight.

Clara gave him a quick rundown of Stephanie's plan and her part in it while Rick listened with raised eyebrows and an occasional groan.

"You took a sizable risk," he said, when she stopped talking. "Did you ever consider that she might kill you?"

"No." She hoped the Quinn Sense would have warned her had that been a real issue, but she could hardly tell him that. "I just feel so bad for Frannie. She suffered so much at Ana's hands, and I know she didn't mean to kill her. She'd just had more than she could take. I hope they go easy on her, that's all."

Rick uttered a soft sound of disbelief. "That woman tried to kill you, Clara!"

"No, she didn't. She just wanted to frighten me so I'd stop trying to find out who killed Ana. She was scared, and I can understand that."

Rick shook his head. "I don't know if I could be that forgiving."

"I just wish I knew what happened to Stephanie." Clara flung a hand out at the empty room. "I left her to wait for me in here. And how did Tim know we were here?"

"It's my guess Stephanie called him. She must have had a good reason to leave."

Clara's nerves snapped to attention again. Just a few minutes ago she'd felt a sense of disaster concerning her cousin. "You're right," she said, and headed for the door leading back into the store. "I'd better call her."

"Guess I'd better get back to my store, too," Rick said, following her out into the darkened aisles. "I left my sister sitting there waiting for me."

Clara paused, looking back at him. "Your sister?"

"Yeah, she came down from Brooklyn for a visit. She'll think I'm some kind of jerk for leaving her alone in an empty hardware store on her first night."

In spite of her concern about Stephanie, Clara felt a little lift in her spirits.

"You should meet Rachel," Rick added, echoing her thoughts. "You two should have a lot in common." He paused at the front door and turned on the lights. "I'll set something up."

The door closed behind him, and realizing she was grinning like a Cheshire cat, Clara wiped the smile off her face.

Stephanie answered on the first ring with a breathless, "Clara! Thank goodness. Are you all right?"

"I'm fine. What happened to you?" Clara listened with growing dismay as Stephanie explained. "Is Olivia all right now?" she asked, when her cousin paused for breath.

"She will be. She's hurting at the moment, but the doctor has given us meds for her. What about you? Did Roberta turn up? Did Tim get there? I called him as soon as I remembered. I feel so —"

"Steffie, I'm fine." Clara told the story for

the second time. "It all worked out, thanks to your plan." She paused, then added, "For once."

"Okay, okay," Stephanie muttered. "I guess I don't exactly have a good track record. How did you know it was Frannie, by the way?"

Clara told her about Frannie's dream. "It was the whale, of course. The charm she'd left to implicate Roberta. In her dream Frannie felt helpless and alone, unable to deal with everything that had happened. She couldn't protect me from the whale. That was her guilt for almost killing me in her attempt to blame Roberta for Ana's murder."

"It's sad, really," Stephanie murmured. "Still, we were lucky that it was Frannie and not some raving lunatic going after the chocolate box. You would have been in real trouble there all alone."

"But I wasn't, and I'm fine and Ana's killer is in custody." Clara let out a long sigh. "I'm just glad it's over."

"Me, too. It was kind of fun, though. Like old times."

"Well, don't get too excited about it. It's not like we'll be making a habit of it."

"Maybe not," Stephanie said, sounding wistful. "But I did like being called Steffie again."

Clara laughed. "Now that's something I can promise to keep up. Just as long as you don't come up with any more of your diabolical plans."

Stephanie's sigh whispered down the line. "No more Quinn Sense, then?"

"No more Quinn Sense."

From out of nowhere, the voice spoke softly in her ear. *Don't bet on it.*

The employees of Thorndike Press hope you have enjoyed this Large Print book. All our Thorndike, Wheeler, and Kennebec Large Print titles are designed for easy reading, and all our books are made to last. Other Thorndike Press Large Print books are available at your library, through selected bookstores, or directly from us.

For information about titles, please call:
    (800) 223-1244

or visit our Web site at:
    http://gale.cengage.com/thorndike

To share your comments, please write:
    Publisher
    Thorndike Press
    10 Water St., Suite 310
    Waterville, ME 04901